"How rare, this delicacy—this calm, sweet, desolated wisdom."

—Helen Garner

"A small pet rabbit takes on greater meaning in this tight, elegant story of a family quartet reckoning with grief. Melanie Cheng captures the claustrophobic, revelatory strangeness of the early days of the Covid lockdown while bravely mining complexities of human emotion—fear, guilt, anger, and love—in lovely, lucid prose that glitters throughout with cut stones of wisdom."

—Lauren Acampora

"Gulped it. I've been a Melanie Cheng fan since our first books came out. But this one is next level—it conveys so much human experience so sparingly that it seems to defy the laws of gravity. Stunning."

—Sarah Krasnostein

"An exquisite portrait of grief and the small things that save us. I was mesmerised."

—Shankari Chandran

"*The Burrow*'s restrained prose and heartbreaking honesty capture the paradox of living with trauma, where the smallest of daily interactions are often the most debilitating. Yet despite dealing with such weighty material, *The Burrow* is an engrossing, compulsive, and uplifting read—a testimony to Cheng's mastery of style and keen insight into human nature."

—Rajia Hassib

"Melanie Cheng's *The Burrow* is stupendously good. This is a novel that deals with the crucial elements of our lives—love and family and grief and guilt and responsibility—and does so without a whiff of sentimentality and does so fearlessly. As in real life, the characters keep surprising us. The power of *The Burrow* is in the unflinching yet empathetic command of the novelist, in the candid beauty of the language. It's a remarkable work, nuanced and human and adult."

—Christos Tsiolkas

Big-hearted and moving, Melanie Cheng's *The Burrow* brings together a family trying to find their way forward in the wake of a devastating loss. Parents Jin and Amy Lee adopt a rabbit for their daughter Lucie in the hopes of restoring a bit of joy to their home in the Australian suburbs, and at first, each family member benefits from the distraction of a new creature in need of care. Things are upended when the arrival of Amy's estranged mother breaks their fragile sense of peace, and the family is forced to confront the terrible circumstances surrounding their tragedy and to ask themselves whether opening their hearts to the rabbit will help them to heal, or only invite further sorrow.

With compassion and a keen eye for detail, Cheng tenderly reveals the lives of others—even a small rabbit—in an unforgettable novel about grief, hope, and forgiveness.

# The Burrow

*a novel*

## Melanie Cheng

TIN HOUSE / PORTLAND, OREGON

Copyright © 2024 by Melanie Cheng
Previously published in Australia by Text Publishing

First US Edition 2024
Printed in the United States of America

Manufacturing by Kingery Printing Company
Interior design by Beth Steidle

Library of Congress Cataloging-in-Publication Data

Names: Cheng, Melanie, author.
Title: The burrow : a novel / Melanie Cheng.
Description: First US edition. | Portland, Oregon : Tin House, 2024.
Identifiers: LCCN 2024025373 | ISBN 9781959030867 (paperback) |
ISBN 9781959030935 (ebook)
Subjects: LCGFT: Domestic fiction. | Novels.
Classification: LCC PR9619.4.C44 B87 2024
LC record available at https://lccn.loc.gov/2024025373

**TIN HOUSE**
2617 NW Thurman Street, Portland, OR 97210
www.tinhouse.com

Distributed by W. W. Norton & Company

1  2  3  4  5  6  7  8  9  0

The most beautiful thing about my burrow is the stillness. Of course, that is deceptive. At any moment it may be shattered and then all will be over.

—FRANZ KAFKA, "THE BURROW"

# The
# Burrow

# JIN

THEY FOUND HIM THROUGH AN ADVERTISE-
ment on Gumtree.

For sale: nine-week-old fawn-coloured male mini lop
in search of his forever home. Lovely temperament, well
handled. Comes with transition feed, nails trimmed,
worm and lice treatment.

The breeder was a hairdresser with a husband in the
army. She laughed when she told Jin she had eleven kids
of her own, as if having that many children were some
kind of joke. She also dismissed the need to immunise
the bunny against calicivirus. "But I'm not an antivaxxer
or anything."

It was the middle of spring. The curfew for metropoli-
tan Melbourne had been lifted but restrictions were still
in place. Now, mid-afternoon, the deserted freeway was
flooded with apricot light. Jin had been driving for forty
minutes, alone, first through country vineyards and later
through graffitied outer suburbs, with the cardboard box

containing the rabbit strapped into the passenger seat. A couple of ragged holes in the lid provided the only airflow. As he drove, he imagined one of the hairdresser's wild-eyed children attacking the box with a sharp stick.

On exiting the freeway and stopping at a set of lights, Jin thought about lifting the lid to check on the thing. The animal hadn't made a sound since they'd left the breeder's ramshackle house. For all Jin knew, he was already dead. Only yesterday, Lucie—who had been researching non-stop ever since he and Amy had caved in to her pleading—had informed him that as little as a dog's bark could give a skittish bunny a heart attack.

But then the lights changed, and Jin turned his attention back to the road, relieved. While he wouldn't admit it to Amy or Lucie, animals made him nervous. He'd never owned a pet as a child. His parents weren't keen about sharing their home with an animal, or even (Jin sometimes thought) a fellow human being. Jin remembered how, soon after they'd migrated, his mother had seen him pat a friend's Labrador on the way home from school and made him take a shower with a giant bar of Dettol soap.

But Lucie had been nagging them. It was the first thing she had shown real enthusiasm about since the accident, and how could they even contemplate depriving the poor child of a pet, after everything she had endured? He and Amy had spent long nights lying side by side in bed, analysing the pros and cons. What if it died? That would be devastating. For her. For all of them. Rabbits were not exactly renowned for their resilience. And a baby one too. *A baby.* On those nights, in the darkness, Jin could tell Amy was weeping—he didn't need to see the tears to know that they were seeping like drops of blood into the soft feathers of her pillow. For a long time, he had been absorbing her sobs like a thready pulse through the mattress.

There was no blood, of course, when Ruby died. In that sense, Jin thought, drowning had to be the cleanest death. By the time he had arrived on the scene, rather than the crumpled, prune-like texture one might expect after such an accident, Ruby's face had a smooth, near-translucent sheen. In the midst of his shock and confusion, Jin noticed the peacefulness of his baby daughter's face—a stillness unaffected by the frantic puffing of lips and frenzied pumping of ribs. When the paramedics arrived to take over the resuscitation, all Jin wanted to do was surrender to that obliteration too.

As he made a left turn, he felt a familiar twinge in the centre of his chest. When the cardiologist had asked him to describe it, Jin had likened the pain to a toothache. If it was an imprecise comparison, it did hint at something truthful—how the sensation resembled the pang of an absence. The incessant gnaw of a cavity or an ulcer or a necrotic wound. A hole, like hunger or homesickness or unrequited love, that insisted on being filled.

Jin pressed the big red button for the hazard lights and pulled over. He killed the engine and leaned his forehead against the steering wheel. Reluctantly, he commenced his breathing exercises. *In, two, three. Out, two, three.*

MELANIE CHENG

*In, two, three. Out, two, three.* During their last visit, the psychologist had told him, in a soft and condescending voice, that breathing would be his new superpower. Jin hadn't booked another appointment. But he had continued with the breathing.

The discomfort eased and Jin leaned back. He still couldn't hear a sound from the box—not a scratch or a whimper or a scuffle. He felt as if he were alone, which offered a kind of relief, until an unwanted image popped up: Lucie's pale face above a furry carcass in the early stages of rigor mortis. He nudged the box and lifted the lid.

Inside was a makeshift nest of hay and shredded newspaper. The rabbit was crouched in one of the corners, making himself very small. For several minutes, he stared at Jin, side-on, through his cartoonishly large eye. He didn't move until Jin extended a finger to stroke him, at which point he shrank even farther into himself to avoid Jin's touch.

Seeing his meaty palm beside the rabbit's cotton-ball head, Jin felt the pain in his chest rise up and burst forth from his mouth in—of all things—a chuckle. He laughed. He laughed because, having witnessed the rabbit in all his naked helplessness, he suddenly found his own fear—of the animal and everything else—absurd. The vulnerable one was in the cardboard box beside him. Jin had a choice, and the animal knew it. He could caress the rabbit's head, or he could snap his tiny neck. Jin removed his hand and closed the lid.

4

When Lucie was a baby, she hated riding in the car and Amy had played classical music to calm her down. Now Jin searched the radio for some soothing instrumental sounds. On finding what he was looking for, he closed his eyes and fell deeply into the music. So deeply, he didn't notice the police motorcycle pull up behind him. It was a surprise to behold the helmeted face like an apparition in the middle of the windscreen. The officer motioned for Jin to roll down the window.

"Sorry, sir," Jin said as he searched for a surgical mask in the glove box.

"Do you have a permit to travel?"

He contemplated showing the officer his hospital lanyard, but then he remembered the bunny. He watched the policeman's eyes scan the cabin and finally settle on the box.

"On my way home after picking up a pet."

The policeman flicked up his visor.

Jin tried to imagine what the officer saw: a slight Chinese man in his early forties with thick hair and panicky eyes.

"I think that's allowed?" Jin continued, desperate to fill the silence. "That it's within the public health orders?"

The officer looked unmoved. "What kind of pet?"

"A rabbit," Jin replied, surprised by the question. "It's for my daughter. Lucie. The rabbit doesn't have a name yet."

The officer shielded his eyes against the sun, which was throwing long beams towards them as it sank behind the trees. "I had a rabbit when I was a kid."

"Oh yeah?" Jin exhaled. There was an unexpected softness in the officer's voice that gave him hope.

"Brutus. I'd wanted a German shepherd, but Mum was anaphylactic to dogs."

Jin suppressed a smile at the thought of a rabbit named Brutus.

"Myxomatosis got him." The officer pulled down his mask to scratch the grooved tip of his nose. "Brought my mates home from school one arvo and when I lifted the lid of the hutch, there he was, stiff as a cricket bat."

Jin wondered if he should convey his condolences, but the pet was so long dead and the conversation so unusual, he couldn't be sure of the etiquette.

"Mum said she was still finding his shit behind the couch, dried and hard as BB bullets, ten years later."

Jin forced a laugh that, when it erupted, sounded more like a cough. The officer threw him a suspicious look.

"Do you have your licence on you?"

Jin retrieved his wallet from his back pocket and pulled out a plastic card.

The policeman gave it a cursory glance. "Go straight home. No more stopping."

"Of course."

Jin watched the policeman ride away before following the motorcycle's bright red tail-light like a guiding star through the empty inner-city streets. As he drove, he practised his breathing exercises and listened to the pounding piano chords of *The Carnival of the Animals*, unsure what or how to feel.

• • • • • • • • •

If he were able, if he were not enveloped in cardboard, the rabbit would have observed the car pulling up in front of a single-storey house blanketed in a bright blue tarp. He would have seen the front yard—a dusty grassless square covered in piles of bricks like burial mounds—and he would have spotted the rosebush with its crimson buds bursting through a nest of thorns. He would have discerned that a light rain was falling and that water was pooling in the dimpled tarpaulin and in the shallow pores of the bricks. His eyes would have been drawn to the only window—a perfect golden square—not shrouded in the bright blue sheet, and he would have started at the silhouette of a small girl with a halo of unbrushed hair. But the rabbit saw none of these things.

• • • • • • • • •

# LUCIE

HE LOOKED DIFFERENT FROM THE PHOTOS. When she looked at him from the side, he didn't even really look like a rabbit, more like some hurried craft project—a couple of tan-coloured pom-poms with two oversized black beads for eyes. Where were his whiskers and his nose? He seemed unfinished, like Ruby when she'd first come home—fleshy and lumpy and unformed. But that hadn't stopped the adults from saying how much she looked like Great Auntie So-and-So and how she had inherited the Lee mouth. Lucie didn't get it. She thought Ruby—in all her doughy formlessness— somehow resembled everybody and nobody at all.

When he had arrived with the rabbit, Lucie's dad had placed the cardboard box on its side on the small patch of grass in their backyard. Lucie had flopped down, belly first, with her head propped up on her hands.

"Open it, Dad!"

The lid had come away to reveal a huddled ball of blond fur in a tangle of yellow hay. Lucie felt her mother crouch beside her and rest a cool hand on her shoulder.

"Don't rush him."

They waited, barely breathing, until he ventured out of his cardboard cave. Lucie watched with silent delight as he took hesitant strides across the grass. Until then, she hadn't known a bunny's nose was constantly twitching— as relentless and tireless as a pulse.

"Rabbits are prey animals," her mum said as they watched him. "They're not like cats and dogs."

As Lucie observed her as-yet-unnamed pet, she imagined an owl nosediving from a nearby tree and whisking the bunny away in its leathery talons. She shook her head to rid herself of the image. Twitching limbs. Cloudy eyes. Matted, metallic-smelling fur.

The family had decided that during the day, when they were home, the rabbit would be free to roam the fenced backyard, but at night, when cats were prowling and birds of prey were hunting, he would be safer inside the hutch. It was a two-storey structure, with an upstairs bedroom and a play area on the ground floor. After a couple of heated arguments, the family had agreed on a location: in the left corner of the backyard, beside the water tank and in front of the shed. For weeks, Lucie had imagined a mini lop bounding through the chipboard arches and scaling the timber ramp. But that first evening (much to Lucie's disappointment) the rabbit had refused to enter his new home. Instead, he'd spent the night in the vandalised cardboard box, placed on the floor of Lucie's room.

The rabbit was always watching, always listening. He was completely in tune with his environment. He was doing everything the soft-spoken man in the mindfulness video had told Lucie to do. Only, the rabbit didn't look relaxed. Not at all. Perhaps, Lucie contemplated, relaxation was just for predators. She had a flashback to a David Attenborough documentary she'd watched once with her dad during the school holidays. She remembered the way the lions had slept, with their legs long and their bellies exposed, and their bulging neck veins on glorious show.

The rabbit didn't like being touched. When she reached out to pat his back, he pulled his body flat against the grass like a cat to avoid her fingers, and when she tried to pick him up, he boxed her with his paws and scratched her with his claws—trimmed to uselessness by the breeder. After a few days, he would permit some brief strokes of his head and nose, but even then, it was a reluctant surrender—a flinch followed by a slow melting of muscles, a hesitant closing of eyes.

At first, Lucie hated him for his hostility. Raw with rejection, she wished she'd nagged her parents for a puppy like every other ten-year-old she knew. With a pang, she remembered the way her grade-two teacher's collie had waited outside 7-Eleven with his eyes wide and his ears pointy with anticipation.

But resentment did not come naturally to Lucie. After she had sulked and ignored the bunny—to no avail, of course—a steeliness evolved somewhere deep inside her. She would make this grumpy creature love her. If it killed her.

# AMY

THEY WATCHED THE RABBIT WITH THE COL-
lective intensity of a family watching a newborn, only
instead of waiting for the flicker of a lip in a weak but
thrilling imitation of a smile, they looked for hops and
flops and a twisted acrobatic leap Lucie called a "binky."
They were the best kind of audience—primed and pleading for rapture. But by far the performance that delighted
them the most was a grooming session, during which the
rabbit rubbed his cheeks with his paws and pulled his
long ears around his face as if in parody of a human being
brushing their hair. Indeed, the act charmed them all so
much, Amy couldn't help but feel it had been choreo-
graphed for their pleasure.

After a few days, however, the novelty wore off. And
when Lucie and Jin returned to their YouTube videos and
newsfeeds, Amy was left to tidy the hutch—a distasteful
task, which involved rolling up the urine-stained newspaper and retrieving stray pellets of poo, sometimes one

at a time between thumb and index finger as if, rather than removing excrement, she were salvaging lost beads from a precious necklace.

On this particular morning, when Amy opened the hutch, the entire contents were soaked through. The small overhang from the shed had failed to shelter the cage from the overnight storm as she and Jin had hoped. Even the newspaper lining the area Lucie called the "bed-room" had disintegrated into a grey papier-mâché mush.

The rabbit looked dishevelled, his fur flattened and dulled by the rain. As Amy watched him shiver before her, she felt a tug of pity as well as annoyance. She retreated to the house to find an old towel and when she returned, to her surprise, the animal let her rub him dry. He didn't even put up a fight when she plucked him from the hutch and placed him in a furry ball on the grass at her feet. He stayed close, grooming himself as she laid down fresh newspaper and hay, and Amy felt a small bloom of satisfaction at this gesture of, if not outright affection, then quiet acceptance.

Lucie found her just as Amy was closing the door to the hutch. Like Jin, her daughter had a knack for arriving at the exact instant a chore was being completed. Amy's eyes fell to Lucie's bare feet on the wet grass. She watched her toes sinking into the soft black soil and tried not to imagine her muddy footprints on the freshly mopped kitchen tiles.

"Mum," she said, looking up with mischievous eyes, "did you know that rabbits eat their own poo?"

Lately, Lucie had been feeding her and Jin these snippets of lagomorphic trivia. Jin was showing signs of impatience, but Amy had yet to grow tired of them.

"They have two types of poos. Hard and soft. They eat the soft type and leave the hard ones to mark their territory."

Amy raised her eyebrows. She was shocked, not by the rabbit's diet but by the girl who stood before her. There was a sparkle in her dark eyes and a pinkness in her lightly freckled cheeks that Amy hadn't seen for a while. Even her hair, a brown, matted mess, appeared to float like something alive.

"I think I've seen him do it. He eats them straight out of his butt!"

At this, Amy and Lucie turned their attention to the hutch. The rabbit stared at them, expressionless, as he champed on a long strand of hay.

"You disgust me, Mr. Rabbit," Lucie said, feigning a scowl.

"Isn't it about time we gave the guy a proper name?"

Lucie drove her big toe even deeper into the earth.

"We can't just keep calling him 'Mr. Rabbit' for all eternity."

"Rabbits only live for five to eight years."

Amy sighed. "You know what I mean."

As she watched her daughter pull her toe from the dirt and survey it—a grubby pink potato—she understood. How many times had Lucie heard her and Jin tell the story? Towards the end (which, of course, they had no idea was the end) it was almost a compulsion. Amy had written a terrible poem about it, even though, really, it was not such an extraordinary tale. But they liked how it made them feel: spontaneous, impulsive, free. Like a completely different family.

*Two clipped and perfect syllables*
*shouted by a toddler*
*at a sonographer*
*across the cool, dark room*
*Ruby*
*ROO-bee*

"How about Dad and I come up with some names, like a short list, and we can make a decision, all three of us?"

Lucie shrugged, but Amy saw the relief in her daughter's face. They walked back to the house together, arm in arm, hopping over the stray bricks and abandoned gardening tools and giggling at the vulgar noises Amy's gumboots made as she pulled them from the wet earth.

It was only later that morning, when Lucie had settled into home schooling, that Amy reflected on what she'd done. Another parent, a *better parent*, would have coaxed the grief from the shadows. A *better parent* would have exposed it. But not Amy. Amy had done what she always did. She had allowed the sorrow to lurk in the wings, gathering strength, while she stood in the open, weakly gesturing at it.

Now, confronted by the blank screen of her computer, Amy tried to steer some of the shame she felt into the novel she had begun to write. But she couldn't even do that. The winking cursor taunted her. How ridiculous to think that while she was working as a medical resident in the hospital, she had fantasised about the life of a writer. She was relieved when her mobile phone vibrated across the desk.

"Hello?"

"May I please speak with Amy Lee?"

The voice was more government bureaucrat than telemarketer.

"Speaking."

"Ms. Lee, I'm calling because you're listed as Pauline Fitzgerald's next of kin."

"What's happened? Is she dead? She's dead, isn't she!"

There was a laugh. "Oh, no! No! Nothing like that. She asked me to call you. She wanted you to know that it was us, meaning the medical team, not her, who suggested we get you involved. She didn't know . . . sometimes it's hard . . . I suppose she wasn't sure what you might say."

"Is she unwell?"

"Oh, no!" That cheery tone again. Amy wondered if she might be speaking to the most upbeat medical intern at work in the pandemic. "She's just broken her wrist. But it's her right one and she's in a cast and the physiotherapist is of the opinion that she's not completely safe to go home."

"I see."

"With COVID circulating, a hospital isn't exactly the safest place for an older person to be, and so we wanted to explore the possibility—"

"Of her coming to stay with us."

"For a short time, yes."

Pauline hadn't been inside the house since the accident, and her stroke, four years ago. She lived thirty minutes away, in the outer eastern suburbs, but that wasn't the reason. Amy still sent her an email at Christmas, and Pauline always sent a gift for Lucie's birthday—a carefully chosen book—but they didn't see each other. Not anymore.

"Ms. Lee? Are you still there?"

"Yes, sorry."

"What do you think?"

"Yes, I meant to say yes. Yes, of course. She's my mother."

# PAULINE

PAULINE'S TAXI PULLED UP IN FRONT OF THE house. Four Cecil Street. She remembered how, a long time ago, Jin had told her that in Chinese culture the number four was thought to bring bad luck. He explained that in Mandarin, the word for the number four was similar to the word for death. She even recalled how Jin had declared, in a slightly patronising way, that he didn't believe in such superstitions—he was a man of reason and science!—and Pauline wondered now if her son-in-law was still the same self-assured man who'd bought this house, with its ominous number, all those years ago.

The driver removed Pauline's suitcase from the boot of the taxi but didn't help wheel it to the door of the house. Instead, he sped away, leaving Pauline at the end of the driveway looking like a bewildered tourist—in a below-elbow cast and a surgical mask. Perhaps if she had worn the sling like the doctors had advised her to, the driver would have helped with her suitcase. But Pauline thought the sling looked ridiculous. She grasped the handle of the suitcase with her left hand and pulled it along the gravel, all the while praying that nobody (most of all, Lucie) was peering through the window and bearing witness to her clumsy incompetence.

The yard was a mess. Pauline had a faint memory of an email from Amy about renovations, but that was years ago. She wondered what all the bricks were for and how long they'd been living beneath the sad-looking tarpaulin. Once at the front door—the one flawless structure amidst the ruins of a veranda in a state of suspended construction or demolition, it was hard to tell—she rang the bell.

Jin answered the door and welcomed Pauline in. Nobody looked at one another. There were exclamations and hugs and pats but no eye contact. They all seemed grateful for the suitcase, which provided an obvious focus for their attention. Jin took it while Amy grabbed Pauline's handbag and Lucie somewhat forcefully ushered her grandmother down the hall.

Pauline knew the house well. She'd spent months pottering within its walls when Lucie was a baby, and once again after Ruby was born. She knew that Lucie's bedroom was at the front of the house, on the left, while Amy and Jin's bedroom was on the right. And she knew that the bathroom—that awful, haunted space—sat behind the one closed door in the hallway.

It was a relief to leave the darkness of the passageway and enter the bright, high-ceilinged living room. Pauline felt as if she could breathe again. She sighed as she sank into the leather recliner and rested her injured wrist on the padded armrest.

"Can I sign your cast?" Lucie asked.

The girl, who had recently turned ten and was not so little anymore—Pauline could see breast buds tenting her T-shirt and detect the slightest whiff of body odour—didn't wait for an answer before going in search of a pen.

Pauline set her face in a placating smile, aware that they were all (except perhaps for Lucie) weary from the sheer effort of their pretension. The room was both familiar and foreign, like something from a dream. Amy and Jin had replaced almost everything, and Pauline supposed she would have done the same. Indeed, she could feel her heart skip a beat as her gaze settled on the one thing they'd permitted themselves to keep: a small pewter-framed photograph, taken days before the accident, of six-year-old Lucie and six-month-old Ruby, with matching pink-cheeked grins.

Lucie returned with a permanent marker and sat down at Pauline's feet to write on the cast.

"How did you do it?" Jin asked, nodding at her wrist.

"It's silly really." Pauline would tell Jin the same fib she had told the doctors at the hospital. "Slippers on a wet floor."

"Ouch."

"Finished!" Lucie declared, replacing the cap on the pen. She had drawn a rabbit beside her name, and a tiny black heart above the letter *i*.

"Cup of tea?" Amy offered, and Pauline saw that her daughter was desperate for an excuse, any excuse, to escape.

"That would be lovely."

She disappeared and Lucie followed, leaving Pauline and Jin sitting at right angles to each another, like doctor and patient, in the middle of the room. Pauline's eyes skimmed the papers scattered across the coffee table—an eclectic collection of Lucie's schoolwork, an overdue electricity notice, and a flowchart for managing COVID-positive patients. In the corner of the room behind the beanbag she spied a dehydrated gummy bear and a dead fly.

"Apologies for the mess."

"Mess? What mess?" Pauline said it to be kind, which was unusual for her, but these were unusual times. She was anxious to show Jin she had changed. She was not the same person he remembered.

"How are your parents?"

Jin seemed surprised by the question, which Pauline took to be a good sign. "Okay, I guess, given the circumstances. They hate the lockdown, of course."

Like Amy, Jin was an only child, and during the twenty years they had been a couple, Pauline had met Jin's parents a handful of times. They lived on the other side of town, in the western suburbs, and were pleasant enough people—painfully polite. Jin's mother always sported a perfect black bob, and his father always wore a tie. But Pauline couldn't help but worry that Amy, in one of her darker moments, had relayed her mother's now much-regretted words—spoken in a feverish haste on the eve of the couple's wedding day—to Jin and his family. If so, Jin was too much of a gentleman to call Pauline out on it, and, perhaps unfairly, Pauline resented his politeness.

"I'm waiting on my friend, Max, to help me fix the roof and veranda out the front, but thankfully we put the finishing touches on the granny flat a couple of weeks before the pandemic hit," Jin said with a smile.

"Perfect timing then," Pauline replied.

They were both grateful when Lucie returned, clutching a terrified rabbit to her chest.

"Look at that!" Pauline said, genuinely delighted by the arrival of the ball of fluff and velveteen ears. Perhaps this was the purpose of pets after all, she thought, to provide a buffer between humans who had forgotten how to talk to one another.

Lucie dropped the creature onto Pauline's lap, where he sat for a few seconds, crouched and very still, before making a frantic leap to the floor.

"What's his name?"

Lucie exchanged a furtive glance with her father. "He doesn't have one."

"He doesn't have one? Isn't that the first thing people do when they get a pet?" She saw shame pass like a cloud across Lucie's face. "How long have you had this bunny with no name?"

"A week."

"A week!"

Lucie hung her head.

"Well, bunny names are easy. Have you ever read *Watership Down*? I mean, is he a Hazel or a Fiver or a Bigwig?"

"What's that?"

"She hasn't read *Watership Down*," Jin interjected, his words short and clipped.

"Well, you really must. I adored it when I was a teenager. I even bought a copy for Amy when she was a kid. Anyway, let's take a look at him."

The three of them stared at the rabbit. His nose twitched furiously. He had the tightly coiled look of a creature who knew he was being watched.

"I would say he's a Fiver," said Pauline.

Lucie's face brightened. "How can you tell?"

"Well, in *Watership Down*, Fiver is the cautious one. But not in an unreasonable way. In fact, he's a little bit magical. A soothsayer. He has strange dreams. Visions of the future."

"Fiver," Lucie said as she squatted on the carpet to scratch the top of her pet's head. "A magical bunny."

Just then, Amy arrived with the tea. Her wary expression told Pauline she had picked up on the altered energy in the room.

"Gran came up with a name!"

"Did she now?" Amy held out the mug of steaming tea. "It's Irish breakfast, hope that's okay."

Pauline felt a stab of pain in her right wrist, like a reprimand, as she reached out with both hands to receive the drink. Oh, if only Amy knew how she'd promised herself over and over again in the taxi that she would be polite and recede into the background and make herself very small. And yet, here she was, within ten minutes of her arrival, naming the new member of the family.

# JIN

IT WAS AN UNSEASONABLY WARM SPRING DAY, and the sun was hot on Jin's T-shirted back. He was reinforcing the rabbit hutch with chicken wire because Lucie had seen a rat prowling the backyard the night before. As he stopped to wipe the sweat from his forehead, he looked over at the rabbit, spread thin as a pelt across a precious patch of shady grass. Jin still thought of him as "the rabbit." He hated his new name, Fiver, which seemed better suited to the offspring of a Hollywood celebrity couple. It didn't help that Pauline had been the one to choose it or that Lucie had been so eager to adopt it.

Jin was surprised by how much he still resented Amy's mother. In her absence, it had been easy to convince himself he'd forgiven her, but now that she was in his house with her overpowering perfume and her loud voice and her bottles of pills lined up like tiny soldiers beside the kitchen sink, Jin found himself yearning for her to acknowledge her part—as involuntary and tragic as it all was—in the complete implosion of his little family.

Distracted by such thoughts, he cut the pulp of his finger instead of the chicken wire. He swore venomously. The rabbit jerked up his head. Jin watched the blood flow from the tiny blossom of splayed skin on his finger before plugging the hole with the tip of his tongue.

Once he had bound the wound up in his handkerchief, he returned to work, watched on by the rabbit. It made him recall a story he'd heard once about an orthopaedic registrar in Hobart who'd been ordered to hand-wash his boss's car every weekend. The worst—or best, depending on one's perspective—bit of the tale was that the boss's children had blown raspberries at him, every Sunday, from their bedroom window on the second floor.

Jin snatched another look at the rabbit. He wasn't blowing raspberries, but he was looking rather relaxed, with his legs and body in a languorous stretch. As irrational as Jin knew it was, he felt irritated. He supposed the decades he'd spent observing his parents' distaste for animals had affected him after all.

Tired, he dropped the wire cutters on the ground and sat down beside the bunny in a slim rectangle of shade cast by the fence. He and the rabbit eyed each other. The creature looked almost sphinx-like with its sand-coloured fur and expressionless face, which made Jin wonder if the ancient Egyptians had kept rabbits as pets. Bored, he pulled out his phone and typed the question into it. Google informed him that hares had been venerated in ancient Egypt for their keen senses and awesome speed.

Just then, Lucie emerged from the house carrying a thick and dog-eared paperback. "Have you finished?"

"Not yet," Jin replied before taking a sip of water from a plastic bottle.

"Can I help?"

Jin remembered his finger, felt its soft throb. "It's dangerous work."

Lucie arranged herself neatly in the trapezoid of shade beside her father.

Jin surveyed the backyard. Thank God the lockdowns had prevented his parents from visiting—they would be horrified by the mess. There were timber planks, bricks, and leftover tiles from the construction of the granny flat that Jin had yet to pack away into the shed. Every so often, Amy would nag him about it and Jin would promise to tidy up, but then it would rain or he would be exhausted after a night shift or he would go outside and stare at the planks and bricks and decide he could use them to build a veggie patch and what was the point of packing everything away only to lug them out again.

Jin's pride and joy was the granny flat, nestled in the far-right corner of the yard. Its bright white walls looked out of place beside the rusted shed and grey fence, but it was this newness that Jin adored. As an emergency doctor, he could only fix things that were already broken—stitching up torn skin, wrapping plaster around fractured bones—but when he had constructed the granny flat with his builder friend, Max, they had created something new and perfect from nothing.

Lucie sighed. She wanted attention.

"What's the book?" Jin asked.

Lucie flashed him the faded cover. "*Watership Down.*"

"The one Gran was talking about?"

"Yep." She flipped through the pages. "This is the copy she bought mum. It's been on our bookshelf all this time."

"Any good?"

"A bit old-fashioned."

"That's not a bad thing."

"Gran says we can read it together. Says she can make sense of it for me."

"Do you like that idea?"

"Yep."

It had always irked Jin how naturally Lucie bonded with Pauline. By contrast, his daughter was stiff and wordless in the presence of her nai nai and yeh yeh. His parents' love had always manifested itself in the buying of gifts rather than the reading of stories—a tactic that worked well when Lucie was a toddler, but not so well when she got to primary school. If anything, once Lucie had turned six, their choice of gifts only served to highlight the depth of the cultural and generational chasm between them. Duplo blocks when she was already constructing Lego masterpieces, plastic Barbie dolls when she had long grown out of them, clothes that were two sizes too big in order to maximise their longevity.

Jin took another sip of the tepid water. He contemplated going back to the house to get a cold drink from the fridge, but he didn't want to disrupt a precious moment: the three of them crouched together on a raft of shade.

"Dad?"

"Hmmm."

"Can people see the future?"

"No." Jin was alarmed by the force and speed of his response. The rabbit hopped around their crossed legs, nudging their thighs with his nose.

"In the book, Fiver sees things. Visions of the future."

"He's a rabbit who can talk, Lucie," Jin said, wiping his brow with the back of his hand. "It's made up."

"But the other day, on Zoom, when we were learning about natural disasters, Mrs. Freeman said animals can sense when an earthquake is coming."

"Those animals aren't seeing the future," Jin explained. "They're tuning into the present. Human beings aren't good at that. We're too caught up in our worries. We're too busy looking at our phones."

Jin remembered the strange way Pauline had stared into nothingness on the morning of her stroke, only hours before Ruby's accident. The vacancy in her blue eyes. He should have done something then. But the episode had been so brief and the signs so subtle and Pauline had seemed so well straight afterwards that Jin had convinced himself it was nothing. He felt another tug of pain in his chest and rubbed the spot with his thumb until the worst of it was gone.

# LUCIE

LUCIE LOVED THE GRANNY FLAT. SHE HAD loved it when it was just a concrete slab in the corner of the backyard—a stage for her plays! a dance floor!— but she especially loved it now. It smelled of new paint, and unlike the rest of the house, it wasn't crowded with old magazines and broken toys. Gran had spent the best part of her first day vacuuming and dusting and polishing her new quarters with her one good arm while, in the main house, Lucie's mum slammed doors and grumbled about the physiotherapist at the hospital needing to have her head examined if she thought Pauline wasn't fit to go home. Gran even cut a few roses from the bush in the front yard and put them in an old jam jar on her bedside table in what she announced was "a finishing touch."

Lucie, who had been reading on Pauline's bed, sat up and looked through the window into the backyard. Her grandmother was approaching along the tributary of concrete that connected the flat to the main house. Lucie imagined her diving face-first into the ground and her forehead cracking open like a coconut shell. Such intrusive visions were usual for Lucie. For as long as she could remember, she had been anticipating fatal accidents. By the time Ruby drowned, Lucie had already imagined her sister's death countless times. Not in a wishful way—not at all! She had loved that baby with her whole heart. But she had also listened to her parents speak about SIDS and seen the way her mother put her ear absurdly close to Ruby's mouth to feel for breathing when she thought nobody was looking.

It wasn't just Ruby. Lucie had envisaged the deaths of everyone. Her mother, her father, her grandparents, her classmates. Nobody was spared. And yet, in spite of her advancing age, Lucie's gran featured the least frequently in such fantasies. If anyone seemed invincible to Lucie, it was her grandmother. In fact, most of the time, Lucie found it hard to believe Pauline and Amy were related. Even now, after her stroke, her grandmother walked with a fixed gaze and bold, purposeful strides. By contrast, Lucie's mother, who had suffered no such stroke, meandered about the house in a random pattern, her pale eyes flitting through rooms and across upturned faces like a pair of insects, settling nowhere.

Lucie sat up and rearranged herself on the pillows in preparation for Pauline's arrival. The door swung open. Pauline kicked off her clogs and lay down on the bed beside her.

"I just put a tray of chocolate chip cookies into the oven. Your mum had some leftover cookie dough at the back of the fridge."

Lucie felt her mouth flush with saliva. "Can you please, please, *please* stay with us forever?"

Pauline laughed and the flimsy bed shook with the strength of her chuckle. "I'm not sure your parents would be so keen on that idea."

Lucie knew her grandmother was probably right, but she didn't want to hurt her feelings and so she said nothing. Thankfully, her gran kept talking. "So, what's happening in the novel?"

"Hazel is getting ready to leave the warren."

"Ah yes, they're finally listening to Fiver."

Lucie put the book on the bedside table and lay flat on the mattress. "Gran, do you believe people can see the future?"

Pauline stared at the ceiling as if the answer could be found there. "I wouldn't rule it out."

Lucie smiled.

Just then the rabbit poked his nose through the door of the flat, which Pauline had left ajar. Together, the girl and the old woman watched the bunny rub his chin along the varnished edge of the doorframe before stepping inside the room. They observed him exploring the area, always cautious, always tentative, but always succumbing to his curiosity. Satisfied, he flopped himself down on a cool tile in a corner of the bathroom.

"I guess he likes your flat too," Lucie whispered.

"It's not my flat."

"Yes, it is."

"Only until my wrist heals. Then it will belong to the lucky person who comes to visit you next."

Lucie stared at the fingernail on her right thumb, ragged from chewing. "Nobody comes to visit us."

"I mean after the lockdown ends."

"And I mean before the lockdown. Nobody came to visit us then."

Pauline stopped whispering. "Your parents have been through a lot." Without removing her eyes from the ceiling, she found Lucie's limp hand on the bedspread and clasped it in her own.

"They don't even listen to music anymore. Sometimes when Mum gets stuck writing her book, she'll play the piano, but it's always those really soft, sad songs and she stops after a few minutes."

Pauline didn't say anything for a while after that. Lucie wondered if she might be crying because she heard her sniff loudly a couple of times, but then Pauline stood up and her face was not the face of someone who had been weeping. If anything, it had a warm pinkish gleam to it.

"What this family needs is a disco party," she announced.

The rabbit, startled, raised his saggy ears.

"What?" Lucie said, even though she'd heard her grandmother just fine.

"We need music. And we need to sing. And we need to dance."

"I have some coloured crepe paper. I could make streamers."

"Perfect."

"And we have some Christmas decorations that look like tiny disco balls."

"Even better."

Just then a voice yelled at them from the other side of the yard. Pauline opened the window.

"Are you guys baking something?"

Pauline and Lucie flashed each other delighted grins.

# AMY

IT HAD BEEN A LONG TIME SINCE ANYONE had baked at 4 Cecil Street. Much to her mother's dismay, Amy had never been great in the kitchen. What had begun as a feminist rebellion during high school—"You're only telling me all this because I'm a girl!"—had morphed into a convenient cover for a lack of talent. But she did love the smell of something warm rising in the oven, and though she would never admit it, the biscuity aroma had nearly brought a tear to her eye that morning.

Amy cried at the most preposterous things nowadays, a predicament that struck her as strange and just a little bit cruel after the long and dry-eyed months and years that had followed Ruby's passing. Oh, how she'd tried to make herself weep during that horrific period—pounding her head against hard surfaces, pinching her skin until her capillaries burst into nebulae of tiny red stars—but the more she willed it to happen, the more impossible it seemed to become.

Not so now. Now, Amy would be driving to pick Lucie up from school and a long-forgotten song would come on the radio—something cheesy like "More Than Words" or "Every Breath You Take"—and instead of the road in front of her, she would see the face of a fleeting crush she'd danced with once at a school disco or kissed during a game of spin the bottle, and before long the tears would be flowing.

Amy sat down at her desk and closed her eyes. She allowed the filtered sunlight to warm her forehead, her chin, her cheeks. Her study had once been the nursery, where first Lucie and then Ruby had slept, and it remained her favourite room in the house. Its north-facing window looked straight onto the backyard, but unlike the kitchen, which bore the brunt of the summer sun, the nursery (which was how Amy still thought of it) was shielded by the eaves and leafy branches of a maple tree.

Most days, this was how Amy spent her time—sitting at her desk with her eyes closed and her face turned to the window, not writing or doing much of anything. She would help Lucie with a few questions about her school-work sometime around ten o'clock—Amy's skills in grade-five mathematics turned out to be embarrassingly poor—before traipsing down the corridor to the kitchen to make a couple of sandwiches for lunch. Months had passed in this way. The deadline for her second book was almost upon her and yet she remained motionless, watching its approach like some large-eyed marsupial in the high beams of a B-double.

Sometimes, instead of sitting at her desk, she would lie down on the floor in the exact spot—still marked by four dents—where the cot had stood. Once there, she would stare at the constellation of glow-in-the-dark stars stuck to the ceiling, now sickly green in the afternoon light. After the accident, she and Jin had discarded as much as they could, but like most things they did, it was reactive and incomplete, and every so often Amy would discover something they'd missed—an absurdly small sock at the back of Lucie's underwear drawer, or a rattle behind the washing machine, or a bib buried in the pocket of an old handbag. And now, instead of throwing these relics away, Amy collected them. There had been a time such punishing reminders seemed to be everywhere and Amy's reflex was to rid herself of them, but now that they were scarce and unexpected, she treated them like pieces of treasure, lifting them to her nose and smelling them, convincing herself that under the mustiness she could still detect a faint scent of baby.

Amy didn't tell Jin about these discoveries. She suspected he would disapprove, or worse, that he would diagnose her with some kind of "pathological grief reaction." Instead, she hid the valuables in an old shoebox at the back of her wardrobe, bringing them out only when she knew he was far away at work.

She resisted any temptation to revisit the box now and turned to her screen. The desire to write had departed with Ruby. Now, the book and everything to do with the book seemed like a terrible self-indulgence. On the rare occasions she had logged on to Twitter to spy on what her writer acquaintances were doing, she'd read their self-deprecating, self-promotional tweets—of the kind she used to post—with a newfound revulsion. By contrast, Jin's work at the hospital seemed far more important. She had even spoken to him about return- ing to medical work herself, but the difficulty of finding someone to look after Lucie had brought an end to that fantasy. Even so, when Amy saw Jin arrive home after a shift, his face still etched with the outline of an N95 mask, his hair still plastered to his ears from the elastic band of the face shield, his lips still chapped and dry from breathing through his mouth, she felt jealous. She, too, wanted to bear the visible wounds of the pandemic. She, too, wanted to feel that she had done something, however small, to contribute. And she continued to envy Jin, even though she knew he felt none of the sense of accomplishment she was craving.

Amy opened her emails. Her publicist had written to request an updated photo to accompany her bio. Amy remembered how much she had adored the photograph on the back cover of her first book. It was her—the same shoulder-length brown hair, heart-shaped face, and thin- lipped mouth—but it was also a stranger. A stranger with intelligent eyes who wrote about intelligent things.

She reached for her phone and turned on the camera. Sunlight was streaming through the window, which was good for photos—the more light, the better, apparently. Some of her writer acquaintances had invested in a ring light for their publicity events on Zoom, which surprised Amy—she had assumed they were above such vanity. Now she held her phone high and cocked her head to the side, mimicking the pose she'd seen others make when taking selfies. But she gave up when she couldn't get her index finger to reach the big red button to take the photo. It didn't matter—she didn't look young or edgy or sexy anyway.

Once, before Ruby was born, Amy had walked in on Jin watching porn on his computer. He was at home following a night shift and Amy had come back early from a meeting in the city. Jin was mortified but Amy didn't care, and they had laughed about it later, in bed together. Amy's sole regret was that she hadn't got a better look at the woman before Jin had slammed his laptop shut—she was curious to see the type of lover her husband fantasised about. Maybe then she would have had an image to accompany the text message she intercepted years later. A rough sketch of the woman Jin addressed only as "M."

She put her phone away and lifted her gaze above the computer and into the backyard. Her eyes found the small mound of the rabbit among the silverbush. As she stared, she could hear the low warble of pigeons and the high-pitched chatter of Lucie in the kitchen. Her daughter's words were muffled but the happiness in them was unmistakable. As much as Amy hated to admit it, having her mother here was a good thing. Lucie had laughed more in the past few days than in the past four years combined. And while Amy had never stopped to consider it before, she now appreciated that, in the wake of the accident, her daughter had not only lost a sister; she had lost a grandparent too.

Being a gran suited Amy's mother in ways that being a mother never had. It was possible Pauline had spent time reading books to Amy as a child, but Amy had no recollection of it. Her childhood memories were dominated by the hot rage she'd felt at her mother's needlessly strict rules and curfews. The "fun grandparent" was a side to Pauline that both thrilled and irritated her.

Just then, she heard whispering and a rustling of papers outside the study. She turned in time to see a rectangle of pink paper being slipped beneath the door. She waited for the retreating patter of feet before leaving her desk to retrieve the sheet, which was, in fact, an invitation.

*Are you ready to get your groove on?*
*Tonight you're invited to an exclusive disco party!*
*RSVP to DJ Lucie*

Amy laid the note across her keyboard. The last thing she felt like doing was dancing. But she was in the habit of pretending. Pretending to be interested in sleep-wake cycles and schools and the impact of screen time on brain development. Pretending to laugh at jokes that made no sense, pretending to be impressed by drawings that were no more than scribbles, pretending to be amused by other parents' "funny" stories from their long weekend trips to the country.

She heard the crunch of Jin's car pulling into the gravel driveway. It was later than she'd thought. The smell of the cookies had been replaced with the scent of something thicker and richer, full of garlic and thyme and tomatoes. In the backyard, the sun began its descent and the rabbit, believing himself to be alone, hopped wild and fast across the grass.

# PAULINE

THE CHILD WAS SO HUNGRY AND SO EAGER and so earnest, it made Pauline incredibly sad. In some ways, Lucie reminded Pauline of herself, not at ten but at the more tender age of five, before she had abandoned all hope in the generosity of adults.

It hadn't always been this way, of course. Lucie had once been an ordinary kid with too many toys and a mother who read her bedtime stories and a father who carried her on his shoulders and gave her tickles that made her laugh so hard she couldn't breathe. But then her six-month-old baby sister had died. And like all children who die, Ruby had left a great big hole in the lives of those who loved her. A hole with an immense gravitational pull—a pull so strong it sucked up all the light.

And so, for Pauline, time spent with her granddaughter was an exercise in self-restraint. Sometimes the urge to tell Lucie to toughen up grew so powerful, she knew it would erupt in a torrent of awful, irretrievable words if she didn't make a quick escape. Tonight, she used the very reasonable excuse of going outside to feed the rabbit some leftover carrot tops while dinner was cooking.

She found him in the silverbush, chewing on leaves. He flashed her that unreadable look he had—an unblinking stare that could signify fear, curiosity, or, worst of all, disdain. But when Pauline set down the vegetables, he pounced on them. He was her fellow animal again then, driven by the same basic needs of water and shelter and food.

As Fiver ate, Pauline took the opportunity to give him a scratch around the ears. She had a habit of loving those who couldn't or wouldn't love her back. She was only ever really interested in Martin, her late ex-husband, when he was having his affairs. Oh, how she had embarrassed herself—bawling and crawling and wailing and flailing— but how in her element she had been then! Because it was only during those upheavals that she had felt truly alive. Desperate and reckless, like a different person. A woman who was willing to sacrifice calmness and control at the altar of something. What a sorry excuse for a feminist she was. If indeed she could call herself a feminist at all. Hating her son-in-law for his coldness when she had chased coldness her entire life. Getting frustrated with her granddaughter for earnestness at the age of ten. *Ten years old!*

As she crouched beside the hutch with her fingers in the rabbit's fur, she felt the prickle of fresh mosquito bites in the skin around her ankles. A possum scaled an electricity pole, its eyes glowing amber in the light from the streetlamp, and a bat screeched overhead before taking roost in the next-door neighbour's fig tree. Pauline wondered what these creatures made of her. If they noticed her at all.

# JIN

JIN SAT IN THE CAR AND WATCHED HIS HOME from the darkness of the driveway. This pause, which Jin had first taken one night after a particularly dreadful shift, had become something of a ritual. Living close to work had its advantages, but the abrupt change of persona from doctor to father was not one of them. To reduce the whiplash, Jin had begun enforcing these periods of stillness. After a while, he found he couldn't do without them. More than that—he enjoyed them. They reminded him of the evening walks he had once taken, as a young teen, between home and violin class—the calm liberation he'd felt as he passed each glimmering window, unseen and unheard, like a small, watchful animal.

Tonight, however, the house looked different. There was a shiny ball hanging from the light on the front porch, and the curtain in the window was drawn. From the car, he could just hear the muffled thud of music and, above that, the occasional tinkle of laughter. Jin could have been forgiven for thinking he'd pulled into the wrong driveway, except that their house was the only one on the street with a giant blue tarp draped like a cloak across its shoulders. Instead, he felt his body stiffen at the prospect of what awaited him.

Pauline had only been with them for four days, but the energy in the house had changed. Not that Jin wanted more of the same. Their lives had become unbearably stagnant, not just since the pandemic began (though that had made things worse), but in the years following Ruby's death. Jin knew stagnation was never a good thing. Stagnant water attracted pests. Stasis within the body caused disease. But Jin had never been good with change. He sometimes wondered if, in another life, he might have become a hoarder—found dead in the last corner of uncluttered space amidst leaning towers of *National Geographic*s.

Jin had agreed with Amy's decision to replace everything after Ruby's death—he was no better equipped than she was to deal with the relentless barrage of memories—but he'd insisted she do it when he was away at work. After Ruby's death he'd experienced a return of some of the magical thinking he'd had as a child. An irrational fear that if he got rid of something, it would somehow invite bad luck into his life. When he was eleven years old, he had dumped his favourite stuffed toy in the donation bin, and within hours he had seen his father doubled over and clawing at his chest, in the throes of a near-fatal heart attack.

At his lowest ebb, Jin would try to identify the missteps he'd made in the twenty-four hours leading up to Ruby's death—a period that took up disproportionate space, like a cancer, inside his brain. If only he'd come home from work five minutes earlier. If only he hadn't stopped to have that coffee. If only he hadn't filled up his car with petrol. If only he'd given her a different name, bought a different house, drunk less, prayed a little. If only he'd taken more care, slowed down, appreciated things. But he had never dared confess such superstitious thinking to Amy. He worried that if he did, she would ask, in that pointed way she had, if it was this fear of making the wrong decision that had caused him to stall on the renovations. Jin wouldn't know what to say.

He looked at the clock on the dashboard. Six minutes past six. He decided that at eight minutes past he would venture inside. He chose eight minutes because eight was a lucky number. But at seven minutes past six, Lucie was at the car window and her face was so ripe with excitement and anticipation, Jin couldn't bear to make her wait any longer. He opened the door and she clambered on top of him, smelling of sweat and tomatoes and brown sugar. Her freckled cheeks were flushed and swollen with a grin.

The entire house felt bright and animated. On seeing him in the doorway holding hands with Lucie, Amy even managed a smile. The kind of smile Jin hadn't seen for a while. Dinner, too, had a carefree air to it. Jin was amazed at what Pauline had been able to pull off with only one good arm, and a little help from Lucie. As was his mother-in-law's style, huge quantities of food were presented in wide ceramic dishes in the middle of the table, which contrasted starkly with Amy's carefully measured aliquots of meat and rice and vegetables. The four of them leaned over one another and bumped elbows and touched fingers as they passed bowls back and forth. Lucie sucked up her spaghetti one strand at a time and the flailing ends splashed tomato sauce over everything, but nobody had the heart to scold her.

As promised, after dinner, Lucie took control of the music. It was clear to Jin that most of the day had been occupied with compiling the disco playlist. He saw Pauline's influence in the inclusion of hits from the Bee Gees and Earth, Wind & Fire, and he saw Amy's touch in the Daft Punk and Jamiroquai and Groove Armada. The adults took turns allowing Lucie to drag them to the impromptu dance floor—a small square of carpet in front of the TV—where they showed off their goofiest moves, initially with hesitation and later with gusto.

As Pauline danced, Jin noticed a slight asymmetry in her smile, a subtle sag in the right corner of her mouth and a smoothing of the skin around her right eye. He had always assumed she'd made a complete recovery from her stroke. This revelation—that she could never experience joy without a tangible reminder of the accident—made him soften towards her.

As for Amy, he delighted in seeing her dance. She had more rhythm than the rest of them put together, and Jin remembered that this had been one of the many things that had attracted him to her in the beginning—the ease and grace with which she moved her body through space. She had stunned everyone at their wedding when she danced the bridal waltz. Even now, as she tried to mimic their exaggerated dance steps, Jin saw that it was impossible for her—she had a natural affinity for the beat. No woman Jin had been with—before their wedding or since—had been able to compete with that.

But then the song ended and Amy's limbs grew straight and stiff and her eyes resumed their aimless roving. The party was over, and they all knew it, in spite of Pauline and Lucie's best efforts to resurrect it with a conga line.

•  •  •  •  •  •  •  •  •

It was the darkest hour of the morning. The moon was hidden behind a cloud. The birds were quiet but the mosquitoes were buzzing and somewhere in the distance a dog barked. The neighbour's tabby was stalking a tiny brown mouse, which circled the hutch before disappearing beneath the fence, while a possum frolicked in the branches of the maple tree—no longer bare but studded with pink buds. Overhead, a tawny frogmouth soared. Only the rabbit was still.

•  •  •  •  •  •  •  •  •

# LUCIE

THERE WAS SOMETHING WRONG WITH FIVER.
After breakfast, when Lucie went to feed him his pellets,
he didn't jump at them like he usually did, and when
she opened the closed part of the hutch where he did
his poos, there was nothing there except a mound of
untouched hay. Fiver sat, crouched in the corner, with
his normally wide eyes half-closed, and made no attempt
to escape when Lucie petted and pulled at his ears.

Lucie ran to the house to report her findings but
paused on hearing raised voices. The long rectangle of
glass in the back door, rippled like a body of water, softened the edges of her parents' figures, but she could still
see the hostility emanating like heat from each of them.
As Lucie turned her back, she caught a few words—
something about their needing to visit Yeh Yeh and Nai
Nai now that the COVID restrictions were easing.

She slumped down on the step, where she would be
safely below the level of the window. Her parents had

woken up feeling buoyed by the news that they would have more freedoms. At breakfast, they'd taken turns to say what they would do first. Amy wanted a coffee at the local café, while Jin was desperate to go to the gym. Lucie, pleased to see her parents happy, pretended to be excited about the return to face-to-face learning.

She looked back towards the hutch and the flat that now housed her grandmother. Perhaps she could tell Gran about Fiver. Gran was both more likely to care and more likely to know what to do than her parents. But Lucie had been instructed by her mum never to wake Gran except in an emergency. Lucie braced herself. She was ten and old enough to decide if this was an emergency. She covered her head with the hood of her dressing gown and walked along the concrete path in her slippers.

Inside the flat, the air felt stale and heavy. She could smell her gran's perfume mingling with the sour odour of the flowers, decaying now in a vase of brown water. Her gran was lying on top of the covers, with one sad-looking breast hanging from the stretched neck of her nightie. Without makeup her face was pale yellow, and gravity had pulled her cheeks into fleshy bags. On seeing her, Lucie felt certain her grandmother had died in the night. But then she heard a faint snore arising from the deep recesses of the old woman's throat.

Lucie stood still and stared into the curtained gloom, unsure what to do. Soon enough, Pauline—sensing her granddaughter's presence—roused. She sat up in bed, and much to Lucie's relief, the rogue breast slipped back inside the nightie.

"Lucie!" she exclaimed, rubbing her face with her good hand.

"Sorry."

Pauline's eyes softened as she sensed the seriousness of the circumstances.

"It's Fiver," Lucie explained.

"What's wrong with him?"

"I'm not sure. He's slower than normal. Weaker. And he hasn't done any poos."

"That's not good."

"I didn't think so."

Pauline took a sip of water from a glass sitting beside the dying flowers.

"Are you mad?"

"Mad? Why on earth would I be mad?"

"For waking you up."

Gran chuckled. "I've slept enough in my lifetime. Besides, this is an emergency."

Pauline pulled on a cardigan and a pair of shoes and she and Lucie stepped out into the garden together. Fiver hadn't moved from where Lucie had found him earlier. Gran made some cooing noises—like the ones she used to make with Ruby—and stroked the rabbit's lowered head.

"He feels hot to me," she said.

Lucie imagined the rats coming for Fiver's dead body. Dozens of tiny furry mouths feeding on his intestines, his heart, his eyeballs.

"What do we do?"

"We speak to your mum and dad about getting him to a vet."

Lucie looked down at her slippered feet. She'd been praying they could sort something out without having to involve her parents. "They're fighting."

Pauline's eyes widened. "Fiver is more important than fighting."

Of course he was. Lucie felt bold as she held her grandmother's hand and retraced her steps towards the main house. She couldn't see the ghostly silhouettes of her parents through the wrinkled glass, but it didn't matter. With her grandmother's protection, she felt ready to face whatever awaited her inside.

# AMY

THE VETERINARY CLINIC SPECIALISING IN rabbits was located on a dead-end road in a nearby suburb. Amy was sitting in her car, on the opposite side of the street, waiting to be called in. Fiver was beside her in his carrier. The lockdown may have ended, but density limits and mask mandates were still in force.

The clinic had insisted on a surname when Amy called to register the rabbit—presumably to distinguish him from all the other animals called Fiver—and so, without thinking too much about it, Amy had used her maiden name. Fiver Fitzgerald. It sounded ridiculous, but she supposed pets' names were supposed to sound ridiculous. As she waited, she could hear the faint sound of the bunny shifting on his bed of newspaper. He knew something was up and the resulting adrenaline had given him a brief burst of energy, which in turn gave Amy hope. She'd spent most of the morning watching him with a ferocious intensity. It would be good to surrender responsibility to someone with actual knowledge about such things.

When she was at medical school with Jin, they had spent several weeks dissecting animals. She remembered the tubs of baby sharks and bins of severed frog legs. All these years later she wondered whether she'd learnt anything during those sessions, other than how to suppress the urge to vomit around wet viscera. But then she'd never been a particularly enthusiastic medical student. She was quite sure Jin, a regular on the dean's honours list, would have some positive spin on the whole thing.

Amy's phone vibrated. The vet was ready for Fiver. She donned her mask and, somewhat inelegantly, extricated the animal carrier from the passenger seat before carrying it into the clinic. The vet, who introduced herself as Lou, was a waif-like being, made to look even more diminutive by her voluminous light grey scrubs.

Lou reached her long, thin arms into the carrier and pulled out a petrified rabbit. Amy was impressed by the way the young woman was able to contain the creature so securely within her grasp. She inspected Fiver's ears and listened to his heart with the bell of her stethoscope. With each manoeuvre she made a thoughtful "hmmm" sound. Then she inserted a thermometer into the rabbit's rectum.

"He's not well."

Amy nodded, suppressing an urge to say something nasty.

"He's febrile and his abdomen is quiet. These are not good signs."

"Is there anything we can do?"

The vet looked at her with serious eyes. "We can run some blood tests."

Amy felt herself bristle. Blood tests would cost money and time, and after the argument that morning, she and Jin and Lucie were supposed to visit Jin's parents the following day. "And what would they tell us?"

"Maybe whether this infection is viral or bacterial."

Amy could tell Lou was starting to get irritated by all the questions. She saw it in the way the sinewy muscles around the young vet's jaw had tightened.

"Can't we just cover our bases and give him the antibiotics?" Amy suggested.

The vet hesitated. "We could."

"Would you mind? It's just that we're supposed to be somewhere tomorrow."

Amy saw the flash of judgment in the vet's anaemic face—Fiver's mummy was no longer just an annoying pet parent, she was a mean and heartless one. But Amy didn't give a shit. The worst thing that could possibly happen to a person had already happened to her. Her heart was thick and callused, and it would take a great deal more than the loss of a pet rabbit she'd known for less than two weeks to upset her.

The vet, anxious to bring the consultation to a close, agreed to give Fiver an intramuscular dose of antibiotics in the clinic on the condition that Amy keep a close eye on him for the next forty-eight hours at home. Amy left with a plastic bag full of syringes, a bottle of oral

antibiotics, vials of an anti-inflammatory called meloxi-
cam, a sachet of "critical-care" feeding solution, and an
invoice for $300.

Once in the car, she put the carrier and the plastic bag
on the passenger seat beside her. The rabbit, exhausted
from all the needles and unwanted handling, was resting
with his eyes closed. Amy stuck her finger through the
bars of the door and scratched his nose.

"Please don't die."

That night, Amy lay beside Jin in bed. His lamp was on
and he was sitting up on a couple of pillows, reading yet
another article about the virus. He was not thrilled about
the vet's instructions. After months of being banned
from visiting his parents, he was determined to see them
this weekend. He had not been swayed by Amy's appeals
to wait for a weekend when he was not on call. Instead,
he had yelled at her, saying that the pandemic had taught
him that waiting only led to regret. Amy suspected he
was also keen to have a break from his mother-in-law.
It had been his suggestion for Pauline to keep vigil over
Fiver while they were away.

"I'm happy to stay," Amy said again, for the fifth or
sixth time. She did not turn to face him but talked to
the ceiling.

"No."

She should have left it there. But she wanted to make
absolutely sure her offer would be remembered. That if
something terrible happened, she would be able to point
to this exchange. "Are you sure she'll be able to manage it?"

"She's pretty good in that below-elbow cast. Probably could have gone home days ago." Jin said all these things without looking away from his computer. Out of the corner of her eye, Amy saw an electron micrographic image of the virus—an otherworldly (and admittedly rather beautiful) fluorescent orb. "Besides, it might do her good, to feel like she's helped us. Healed something."

"And what if he doesn't heal?"

Jin closed his laptop and placed it on the floor. "I don't know, Amy. I don't have all the answers. But if he does end up dying, maybe it's better that it's your mother who cares for him. After all, she can run away when everything turns to shit. God knows, she's done it before."

"We never should have got that rabbit."

Jin breathed in and out three times. "Maybe not."

Amy wondered how Fiver was doing. After much negotiation, they'd agreed to put him in a playpen in Lucie's room for the night.

"When Lucie was born," Amy began, "I would creep into the nursery to check that she was still breathing."

"So would I."

"Every night I braced myself to find her unresponsive."

"Amy—"

"Years later, I did the same with Ruby. And yet, Ruby's death caught me by complete surprise. I'd never imagined anything like that. I was unprepared for it. I felt like a passenger taking a piss in the toilet when their plane hurtles to the ground."

"Is this helpful?"

"Is anything?"

Jin went to the bathroom, brushed his teeth. When he got back into bed, he'd softened. "It's the same with my patients. I spend too much time worrying about the wrong things."

Amy gripped the blanket with both fists. "It didn't protect them."

"You don't know that."

"I wish, instead of creeping in to check on her every night, instead of listening to her breathing in the dark, I'd picked her up and brought her into my bed and held her close and never let her out of my sight."

Jin was quiet for a long time again after that. So long that Amy found it hard to tell where the silence ended and the sleep began.

# PAULINE

IT WAS EARLY AFTERNOON. AMY, JIN, AND
Lucie had departed straight after breakfast. It was a forty-
minute drive to Jin's parents' place, and Jin wanted to spend
the whole day there. The house was quiet without them—
unbearably so. For decades, Pauline had lived quite happily
on her own, and yet now, after only a week of living with
others, she was acutely attuned to—indeed, disturbed
by—the absence of sound. She found herself anticipating
the pad of Lucie's feet on the timber floorboards or the
growl of the coffee machine in the kitchen. In the end,
she retreated to the cosy claustrophobia of the granny flat,
taking Fiver with her and laying a bed of newspaper and
towels for him in the corner.

As much as Pauline hated to admit it, she was impressed
with the aptly named "granny flat." She knew Jin, with
the guidance of his friend Max, had laid every brick
himself, and though Pauline was not a builder and had
no experience of such things, she could tell that it was a

solid, reliable structure. She knew this because at night, when she closed the window and the door, there were no rogue whistles or streams of cold air on her face. Jin's perfectionism showed in the neat lines and sharp corners of the room, and she wondered if it was this meticulousness—it must have exhausted him—that had stopped him from finishing the front of the house.

Pauline was not a perfectionist. She liked a tidy home, but she didn't care if the linen cupboard was bursting with crumpled sheets, or the drawers were full of useless, broken things. She was happy as long as she could cast her eyes across a room without them snagging on a cobweb or a dirty sock.

Only that morning, after the family left, she had tidied Fiver's hutch, deriving untold satisfaction from the sight of clean newspaper and bowls of fresh pellets and water. Not that he would be needing the hutch tonight. Pauline had been given explicit instructions by Lucie—and less explicit but equally emphatic instructions by Amy—not to leave the rabbit's side. They were both careful with their words, but Pauline sensed their anxiety.

She looked over at Fiver in a puddle of sunlight beneath the window, rendered calm and compliant by illness—in this sense at least, he did resemble a small child. Today, rather than tolerate Pauline's pats and rubs, he seemed to enjoy them. Earlier, the rabbit had even allowed Pauline to pick him up, and Pauline, in turn, had relished the weight of him on her lap, the feel of his fur on her fingers.

Not long ago, Pauline had read about a project in Japan trialling the use of mechanised baby seals in aged-care homes. At the time she had worried that physical contact was just the latest human need to be outsourced to a machine. And yet today, when Fiver had rested briefly in her arms, she had been able to appreciate the healing potential of something soft and warm and weighty on her body. She'd read another article—she was forever reading them, there were so many!—about the comfort of simply holding a mug of tea. The writer said it was this heat—on our palms and our cheeks—rather than anything nourishing in the brew itself, that drew us to turn on the kettle.

Every few hours, Pauline syringed a few millilitres of the critical-care solution—which looked less like medicine and more like a child's potion of pulped grass—into the corner of the rabbit's tiny pink mouth. It was no small feat, holding the animal with her plastered arm and using her left hand to administer the liquid. When she was done, she wiped the spillage from his fur with a wet face towel as if he were a baby.

When he slept, in small frequent bursts throughout the day, Pauline lay on her bed and read *Watership Down*. She hadn't picked the book up since she was a teenager, and she found re-reading it disorienting. As an idealistic adolescent, she had been immersed in the epic story of an odd group of rabbits and their quest to establish a thriving warren, but now she responded with cynicism. She *expected* the violence between the dominant bucks—she expected more.

Disappointed, Pauline put the book back on her bedside table. The rabbit was asleep, flopped on his side with belly exposed. He never slept for very long, but then Pauline supposed prey animals had no choice. How awful to be pursued and lusted after in that way. How utterly exhausting. Pauline felt a drag on all her muscles and bones at the thought of it.

# JIN

DINNER WITH HIS PARENTS WAS CUT SHORT by a call from the head of the emergency department. It was six thirty on Saturday night and the weekend was over. "A few doctors have called in sick," the consultant said. "Can you please step in?" Jin knew the pleasantries were for show. He had no choice in the matter. At the hospital, you didn't say no to your boss.

They had driven two cars to his parents' house in anticipation of this exact scenario, and as Jin retrieved his keys from Amy's handbag, he avoided her eyes, which he knew would be alight with rage at being left behind with his parents. Lucie looked miserable, using her chopsticks to push a chicken bone around her bowl as Nai Nai asked her how she was doing at school—had she memorised all her times tables yet? Did she know how to do long multiplication and division? Had her dad told her that he had won a prize for algebra when he was ten? Did she hope to be good at that too?

How could Jin explain to Lucie that one day, when she was much older, she would become curious about his parents? That—as impossible as it was to imagine now—she would see traits in her personality and features in her face that were not from him or Amy but from them? That they were part of the tiny group of people who would always remember and grieve for Ruby?

It was a relief for Jin to escape. There weren't many places left where he could feel at peace. Not in his parents' home, where Amy and Lucie made their displeasure known. Not in his own home, where Pauline's perfume and her freshly baked goods and her bowls of potpourri had infused everything. Not at work, where his colleagues, muzzled by duck-billed masks, attempted to communicate through plastic-wrapped eyes: an eye-roll, a raised eyebrow, a panicked *get me outta here* stare.

As Jin drove down the wide, tree-lined boulevard to the hospital, he found some jazz on a community radio station. It was the kind of amelodic, agitated music that he ordinarily found tedious. Tonight, however, it suited his mood. He was feeling almost content when he pulled into the hospital's underground carpark just after seven thirty.

At this time of night, the emergency room practised a no-frills kind of medicine. Patients were classified into one of two categories: emergencies, and problems that could wait until morning. Even as a terrified junior doctor—acutely aware of the danger posed by a skeleton staff and the tendency for pathology to flare after sunset—Jin was energised by the unpredictability and hot, pumping adrenaline of a night shift.

But any contentment or anticipation was shattered by the apparition of Mindy in front of his car. She was standing with arms outstretched in a pose that might have been dramatic if Jin had been travelling at a speed greater than ten kilometres per hour.

When he put his foot on the brake, Mindy made her way around to the passenger side. She didn't ask permission before opening the door and collapsing into the seat beside him.

"I thought I'd never see you again," she said, tearing off her mask. Her lipstick was red and flawless.

Jin wound down the window. It was suddenly unbearably hot and airless inside the cabin. "We work at the same hospital. It was bound to happen."

Mindy laughed. Her black bob bounced around her head. "I know. And yet our paths haven't crossed for months. It was approaching a statistical impossibility."

Jin felt his cheeks burn. In early winter he had put in a discreet request not to be rostered on any shifts with Mindy.

"It's a global pandemic, Mindy. Statistically improbable things are happening all the time."

"True," Mindy conceded and laid her perfectly manicured hand, so small and warm compared to Amy's, at the top of his thigh.

Jin flicked it away, as if, rather than a hand, it were a spider. "This was wrong before. I think it might be illegal now."

Mindy chuckled again and Jin was struck by how incorrigible she was. It was a trait Jin had enjoyed in the beginning (she was so different from Amy!) but that he now recognised as a particularly dangerous characteristic—for him.

"I've been thinking about all the affairs that must have ground to a halt after the lockdown."

"Ours ended well before that."

"Did it? I seem to recall a relapse . . ."

That did it. Jin pulled into a parking spot and killed the engine. In the dimmed cabin, Mindy's sharp-edged face took on a sallow tone. He was repulsed by her.

"Get out."

"You've got my number."

"Get out."

When she was gone, he could still smell her perfume, which was neither citrusy like Amy's fragrance nor flowery like his mother-in-law's eau de toilette. It was a smell unlike anything Jin had encountered before. It was all Mindy: excessive, saccharine, sharp. He felt hot bile lap the back of his throat. And yet . . . like some Pavlovian dog, he also felt an involuntary (and slightly painful) fullness in his crotch. How he hated his body then. He stuck his head out the window and took hungry gulps of the stale, fume-laden air. Mercifully, his cock softened. When he got out of his car and pulled a surgical mask from his bag, he was relieved to have an excuse to cover his face.

# LUCIE

THEY HAD STAYED ONLY ANOTHER HALF AN hour at Nai Nai's house after her dad left—it was intolerable when he wasn't there to shield Lucie from their probing questions. Lucie knew Nai Nai and Yeh Yeh were as relieved as she was when Amy declared they were going home.

A light rain was falling as they drove along the freeway. Her mum was a slow driver compared to her dad, but that didn't stop Lucie from imagining all the horrific accidents they could have. Her blank—almost serene—expression gave nothing away, but her brain was piling on the images of her mother: pinned beneath the crumpled carcass of their Volkswagen, flattened beyond recognition by a semi-trailer, coiled in the emergency lane with blood pouring out of her nose.

When her dad wasn't around, Lucie sat in the front passenger seat, beside her mum, which made her feel grown-up. Sometimes, they would listen to the radio and a song would come on that reminded Amy of her youth, and she would tell Lucie about her first slow dance at the school disco, or a hair-raising bus ride in Brazil, or a full moon party in Thailand, and she would get that faraway look in her eyes.

"Mum," Lucie said, "did you know that rabbits don't cry?"

"I didn't know that," her mother replied.

"I searched it up."

"What do rabbits do when they get sad then?"

"They stop eating and sleeping," Lucie said, trying to recall what else the website had mentioned. "They hide and stay very still."

When they got home, around eight, Pauline led Amy and Lucie through to the backyard, where Fiver was nibbling at a silverbush, illuminated by the spotlight above the shed. Lucie felt her tear ducts prickle with delight, and when she looked up, she saw her happiness reflected in her mother's smile.

"He started perking up in the last half an hour or so," said Pauline.

"What a relief," said Amy.

Lucie said nothing on account of the ball in her throat. She kneeled down on the grass and stroked Fiver's cheek.

"And you managed okay?" Amy asked.

"Fine."

Lucie tuned in to the soft crunching noise made by the rabbit as he chewed on dried leaves.

"You'll be wanting to go home soon, I suppose," Amy said finally.

Lucie kept patting the bunny, but she could feel the joy of only a moment before leaching from her insides.

"I've still got a few weeks left in the cast," Pauline said. "But I was fine today while you were away."

From her position in front of them on the ground, Lucie couldn't see Pauline or Amy, but she could hear them. Gran's voice sounded cheerful enough, but Lucie wished she could search her grandmother's face for some sadness, a sign that—in spite of her play at being brave— she wanted to stay.

"I'm sure you all miss having your own space."

Amy said nothing and crouched beside Lucie. She feigned interest in Fiver and pretended to feed him more leaves. Oh, how Lucie hated her mother then.

"Gran?" she said, standing up and taking Pauline's hand.

"Yes, honey?"

"Will you read me some more of *Watership Down*?"

"Of course."

"It's late," Amy warned, "nearly your bedtime."

But Lucie ignored her and pulled Pauline towards the granny flat, with Fiver bounding close behind them.

# AMY

AMY DID NOT WANT TO DEPRIVE HER MOTHER of joy. It was just that if Pauline healed—after everything that had happened—there would be an expectation that Amy's recovery would soon follow. And Amy wasn't ready for that. She wasn't ready to let go of the little nub behind her sternum, the invisible scar that pulled and puckered with every movement, tugging her back towards her sorrow.

Amy knew she needed to be more *engaged*, more *present*, in her interactions with Lucie. She knew this because it was what the child psychologist had told her. But Amy's brain was no longer an obedient instrument. It no longer felt entire. It was as if a part of it had departed with Ruby. The good part. The intelligent part. The fun part. The part that remembered things and fixed things. The part that, at least occasionally, knew what to do.

She scratched her ankle. She must have been bitten when she was outside feigning admiration of her mother-in-law's bougainvillea. The itch reminded her of the mosquito netting Lucie had insisted they pick up from the hardware store on the way home. In her extensive research, Lucie had discovered that mosquitoes were a serious, perhaps even *the single most* serious, danger to domestic rabbits. And so, while the bars on the hutch would keep the cats and foxes out and the layer of chicken wire would stop the rats from getting in, they needed yet finer protection to prevent an influx of the tiniest and most deadly of predators.

Amy retrieved the netting from the boot of the car, which was parked on the street behind the house. As she came through the gate in the back fence, she spied Lucie and Pauline through the window of the granny flat, lying on Pauline's bed reading *Watership Down*. Lucie was holding the book above her head with her arms out straight, a position that, given its heft, must have been painful. But if Lucie was feeling any discomfort, she wasn't showing it. She looked enthralled.

The cheapest netting they'd managed to find was a canopy, the kind that hung above beds in malaria-prone countries or, in places where air conditioning and sealed windows locked mosquitoes out, above little girls' beds. "Princess beds" they were called, but Lucie didn't want one for herself. Amy screwed a hook into the timber awning of the shed and threaded the string hoop attached to the top of the canopy through its eye. She proceeded to arrange the excess mesh around the perimeter of the hutch as if it were the billowing skirt of a wedding dress.

When she stood back to appraise her work, she was struck by the absurdity of what she was doing. All these nets and wires and filigree solutions. For what? The protection of a prey animal who, in the wild, would simply bury himself in the ground.

Her thoughts turned to how she and Jin had baby-proofed the house when Lucie had first started crawling. The plastic plugs inserted into every power socket. The foam padding attached to the corners of every table. The metal gates—painted white to make them look less like prison bars—erected at the entrance of each room. She and Jin had intended to remove these protections when Lucie was older, but then Amy had fallen pregnant again and it made sense to leave them in place. How stupid, Amy thought now, how incredibly deluded.

When Jin arrived home, sometime before dawn, he reached for Amy in the dark. It was the first time in a long time, but Amy couldn't find it in herself to respond to his touch. As he slipped his hand up her pyjama top and his fingers found the warm bud of her nipple, her body recoiled. Jin, understanding, pulled her pyjama top back down to cover her belly. He rolled onto his side, resuming the left lateral position. The safest position—or so Amy had been taught during first-aid training—for the unconscious person.

"Do you remember," Amy began, hating herself with every word, "how, when we first went out, we got tired of saying 'I love you'? How we felt it was so overused? How we looked for new ways to say 'I love you' to each other?"

"I'm tired, Amy."

"Do you remember what we used instead?"

"Amy—"

"'Wawa.' It was from one of the African countries, I think. It wasn't ours, of course. It was probably appropriation. But we thought it was cute. Until we used it in public. And then it just sounded like we were cooing to each other. Like lovesick babies. Which I suppose we were."

"What's the point of this?"

Couldn't he see? It was her way of telling him she still loved him without saying so—without throwing open her legs and actually making love to him.

At the very least, it got his attention. He was no longer lying on his side but propped up on his elbows, facing her with a sombre expression. "Do you realise you only ever talk about the past?"

*Do you realise*, she wanted to shout, *it takes all my energy to fish these tender morsels out of my brain?* But she didn't say this. Instead, she said, "I watched a documentary once about the space-time continuum. A physicist was trying to explain that time is not linear, even though human beings experience it that way. He used the example of when we travel from one place to another—how, when we arrive in a foreign city, we believe that our home still exists, even though we can't see it or feel it or be in it. He said the past is like that, that it exists alongside the present. Like another city. Another room."

"A locked room."

"Perhaps."

Jin was lying on his side again now, his back a block of shadow. "You know, Amy, the past isn't some perfect thing like you make it out to be. It was unpleasant and flawed and pretty fucked up if I'm going to be honest about it. Sure, looking back now, after everything that's happened, those problems seem like stupid, irrelevant distractions, but we didn't have that perspective then. We were often angry. We were often bored."

How she longed to reach out to him then, wrap her arm around his chest, pull him towards her, fuck him. Instead, she mirrored the arc of his body, close but not quite touching. A pair of lovers, safe, but each hopelessly alone, in the left lateral position.

# PAULINE

PAULINE HAD BEEN AT HOME WHEN SHE BROKE her wrist. Another fall in another bathroom. She'd used her left hand to call triple zero, and when the paramedics arrived, she'd told them she'd slipped on the wet tiles. The truth was, she couldn't remember what had happened. She couldn't even recall walking to the bathroom. She only knew that when she woke up, her pyjamas were soaked with urine and her right arm was hot and throbbing. In the twenty minutes it took the ambulance to arrive, Pauline swallowed two ibuprofen tablets, changed into a fresh pair of tracksuit pants, and packed a small suitcase for the hospital. If these strokes wouldn't put her out of her misery, she would make goddamned sure she maintained her dignity.

She'd anticipated it would be a short stay—she'd never imagined she would end up living with Amy—and so she had brought only the essentials: a toothbrush, a nightie, three pairs of undies, slippers, a change of clothes, a house dress, something warm. It had taken her all of five minutes to pack, one-handed, and now her bag looked small and sad, like a lost child, in the middle of the bed.

She would go home in the morning. After Amy's comments the previous night, she couldn't possibly stay. The physiotherapist at the hospital had never specified how long she would need help for—Pauline suspected they were just relieved she had become someone else's problem—and there was really nothing she couldn't do with the cast on.

Only Amy was aware of her plan. She would tell the others over breakfast. Pauline knew this was selfish, but the less time she had to spend looking at Lucie's big, sorrowful eyes, the better. Dinner had been an awkward affair of exaggerated pleasantries and stilted conversation. Jin seemed weary and preoccupied, while Lucie fed them rabbit facts from her apparently endless repository. As the family chewed on their chicken drumsticks, she informed them—with what Pauline thought was a twinkle in her eye—that female rabbits could reabsorb their embryos when the warren got too crowded.

Pauline had spent the remainder of the meal grappling with this new information. She felt both repulsed and fascinated by this blurring of boundaries between mother and child. She couldn't help but wonder if the doe was forever altered by the resorption of her baby or if, as with other forms of consumption—eating and drinking—she simply extracted the nutrients she needed and let the rest filter through her.

Now everybody had retired to their rooms and the main house was dark. Pauline remembered how as a young mum she'd loved being the last one to fall asleep. There had been a sense of relief in it, of course, but also a sense of freedom. Mostly, she would do nothing more shocking than down a diazepam with a few glasses of shiraz, but in those precious liminal hours everything seemed possible. Sometimes she fantasised about nipping out to a local jazz club and kissing a long-haired musician, hard, in the back of a graffitied toilet cubicle, before making it back home in time to cook breakfast for Martin and Amy in the morning.

She changed into her nightie and moved the bag to the floor before climbing into bed. She was not looking forward to going home. She would miss her grand-daughter and she would miss the rabbit and she would miss the push-and-pull of human beings orbiting one another like tiny planets. But such thoughts were not helping her get to sleep. She needed to quiet her mind. She focused on the tension in her muscles and the way her body was moulding to the mattress—her heels and the back of her skull sinking the deepest, followed by her bottom and shoulders and finally her limbs. She became aware of the way she was holding her face in a slight scowl. She forced herself to take notice of her breathing, tame it, slow it down.

She was in an early, shallow phase of sleep when a noise punctured the silence. At first, she dismissed it as the scuffling of yet another pesky possum, but then she heard the doorknob rattle. It was the first night Pauline had locked the door of the granny flat. She wasn't sure what had made her do it. Perhaps it was a last-ditch attempt to establish a boundary—a little unspoken *fuck you* to Amy. Whatever the reason, Pauline was glad of it as she lay, silent and still, in the darkness.

When she heard the crunch of feet on dry leaves, she knew the intruder was at the window. Only yesterday, she'd noticed the leaf litter and made a mental note to get rid of it. She held her breath, listened. Could that squeaky noise be the sound of a wet finger sliding down the glass? It wasn't raining. Could it be that he was sweating? Could it be that he—because surely it was a he?—was nervous? As terrified as she?

Pauline reached for her phone on the bedside table, pulled her head beneath the covers. Once she'd steadied her trembling fingers, she sent a message to Amy.

*Man in backyard. Call the police.*

Pauline waited for Amy to read the message. She saw the three pulsing dots, but no reply came. Once again, the doorknob to the flat shook, only this time it was more of a shudder.

The brick came through the window at the exact moment Jin yelled out from the back door. To Pauline's ears, the noises were indistinguishable from each other, like sections of a climaxing orchestra. The melodic tinkle of shattered glass and the brass boom of Jin's bellow.

The intruder was gone by the time they'd come to their senses and were able to take in any meaningful details. As they regrouped in the kitchen around cups of untouched tea, they compared notes. Pauline thought she'd spotted a smallish person in a dark green hoodie, possibly a teenager, scaling the back fence, while Jin said he'd seen someone taller and slimmer with black hair. Lucie was adamant the prowler was wearing a beanie, while Amy thought the flash of a ponytail favoured a girl.

Either way, their descriptions were completely contaminated by the time the police officers from the local station—a couple of stern young women—attended the scene. Not that it mattered. With no CCTV cameras and no damage to property other than the broken window, the officers didn't hold much hope of finding the culprit.

"We'll file a report. Take a few photos. Fingerprint the door handle."

"Have there been other . . . incidents?" Pauline asked, mindful of her words in front of Lucie.

The less stern of the two officers smiled. "A few kids have been out creating trouble. Letting off steam after the lockdown."

"So it's random?" Jin said. It was the first question he'd asked since the police arrived.

"Oh yes, it's almost certainly random. We see this kind of thing all the time."

When the officers left, sometime around 2:00 AM, a weighty, terrified silence descended upon the kitchen. They were tired, more tired than they'd been in years, but they were also too agitated to sleep.

"You'll have to move inside," Jin said to Pauline. "We can put an extra mattress in Amy's study."

Pauline had been so preoccupied, she hadn't considered the sleeping arrangements. She was grateful Jin was the one to invite her, unprompted, without needing to consult Amy.

"Can Gran sleep in my room instead?" Lucie implored in a soft voice from the other side of the kitchen table.

"I'm sure your grandmother's tired," Jin said, but he and Amy joined Lucie in a silent plea.

"Of course."

The family got to work, blowing up the inflatable mattress, collecting fresh linen from the cupboard, putting cases on pillows. They worked in quiet unison, almost in a dance, intent on ignoring the prowler who, though absent, continued to haunt them. They were so distracted that none of them turned their thoughts to the rabbit, encased in his layers of protective netting, alone in the dark, outside. It was Lucie who woke with a start, an hour or so later, screaming his name—"Fiver! Fiver! Fiver!"—at which point Pauline patted and shooshed her back to sleep as if the events of the night were all a terrible dream.

# JIN

IT SEEMED LIKE A BIG DECISION, AND SO JIN thought about it for a long time. Many people walked past him while he stood in the alleyway beside the house, staring at the brick wall. Some were walking their dogs, and they picked up their dogs' shit in tiny green bags worn inside out, like gloves. Most were masked or donned one on spotting Jin with his serious eyes and crossed arms.

If only, Jin thought, he could keep guard around the clock. Surely that would stop people from breaking the rules, from breaking into other people's houses, from breaking their windows. But of course he couldn't do that. He had to eat and sleep and work. And in the meantime, these dummy cameras from the hardware store would have to suffice—at least until he could get an electrician to wire up a ludicrously expensive security system—which brought him back to the crucial decision of where to place the damned things. He had bought

two. One would have seemed half-hearted; three, para-
noid. Two, in Jin's opinion, was the Goldilocks number.

The house was flanked by two laneways, one at the
rear and one at the side. The backyard was separated
from the rear alley by a gated fence, while a brick wall
ran along the alley on the right. The brick wall was plastered with indecipherable tags in dripping hot pink letters. Jin hoped that, in addition to deterring intruders,
the cameras would put a stop to all the graffiti. But two
cameras posed their own problems. If he placed them too
far apart, there would be a blind spot in the middle. The
angles were important too—no good snapping, or pretending to snap, images of a lot of feet.

Jin hadn't slept a wink the night of the invasion. In the
dark cocoon of his bedroom, he couldn't shake a disturbing, if absurd, thought—that the intruder was actually
Mindy, come to enact her revenge. It was ridiculous, of
course. He chided himself: *Your life is not* Fatal Attrac-
tion*; Mindy doesn't care about you that much.* But he
couldn't make it stop.

As he fought these silent battles, he heard Amy shift in
the sheets beside him. At 4:00 AM, when she got up, he
should have said something—some words of comfort or
reassurance or even a joke about their shared insomnia—
but he felt inadequate. After all, Pauline had messaged
*Amy*, not him, about the intruder. And Amy had taken
control of everything—jumping up to peer out the window, calling the police. It was as if Jin had become invisible or inanimate or, perhaps worst of all, a child. When

he rushed to the back door to shout at the intruder, it was as much to remind everyone, including himself, that he had a voice at all. And then the brick had erupted through the glass, and, horrifyingly, the smallest amount of urine had leaked onto Jin's underwear—not enough to give him away, just enough to make sure he knew what a coward he was.

Until the accident, Jin had never felt the need to play the role of protector. He'd always considered himself progressive, open-minded, a feminist. It was just that, ever since Ruby died, Amy and Lucie had lost faith in him. He was an emergency physician and he had failed during the greatest emergency of their lives. In addition to all the obvious things the accident had taken from him— his child, his happiness, his trust in the universe—it had also deprived him of any hint of satisfaction with his job. He had become a follower of procedures. An automaton. Which was probably better for the patients, who had more to gain from a clear-thinking robot than from someone whose judgment was clouded with feeling, but Jin missed the sensation of being emotionally invested in an outcome. He missed the fear and the worry. He missed *caring* about something.

Neighbours continued to pass him in the alleyway. The lockdown might have been over, but many were still wary of the virus. Jin said hello to a few people he knew. Mothers and fathers he recognised from school, the grumpy man who owned the milk bar, the nonna with the corgi sporting brightly coloured knits. He and Amy had lived in this gentrified inner-city neighbourhood for almost ten years, and yet Jin didn't feel as if he belonged here. As much as he hated to admit it, he felt more at ease in the western suburbs, where his parents still ran a post office, than in his adopted home.

It had been Amy's choice to live where they did. It suited her to be close to theatres and bookstores. To be fair, Jin enjoyed the abundance of cafés and bars in the area too. But once Lucie had started school, he felt like the newest guest at a never-ending dinner party.

Lockdown had provided a reprieve for both him and Amy. There was a relief in not having to create excuses to avoid trivia nights and after-work drinks. There was a paradoxical sense of freedom in not having to make all the decisions for once. Decisions that somehow felt both frivolous and pivotal at the same time. Decisions that didn't really feel like decisions at all. Decisions like where to place two dummy cameras on a large brick wall.

# LUCIE

NOTHING WAS THE SAME. IT WAS AS IF THE bubble they'd been living in for the past week had burst along with the glass in the window. The glazier had come and gone. Shards had been swept away. But her mum was more depressed than usual (Lucie hadn't thought it possible), her grandmother was jumpy, and her dad spent all his spare time online, researching home security systems. Lucie had begrudgingly returned to school, and for the past two nights, she'd wet the bed.

Even the rabbit was different. At first, Lucie thought she might be imagining it. It was afternoon and the light was glary in the backyard. But then he started chewing his pellets and its presence was undeniable. A subtle asymmetry in his face. Lucie couldn't work out which was normal—the puffy cheek or the sunken one.

"Is he eating?"

"Yes."

"Pooing?"

"Yes."

"Sleeping?"

"Yes."

"Well, he's a happy, healthy rabbit then."

Moments earlier, Lucie had dragged Pauline from the kitchen, where she had been busy preparing dinner, to the hutch, where the rabbit was now resting on the bottom floor.

"But look at him!" Lucie implored, and she must have had just the right amount of whining in her voice to convince her grandmother to take another look. Pauline kneeled down beside Lucie and peered into the rabbit's home.

The longer Lucie stared, the more obvious the deformity became. Before her eyes, what she had discounted as a trick of the mind became the first telltale sign of a debilitating—and possibly fatal—disease. She didn't know what cancer looked like, only that her mum had had several spots cut out from the skin on her back and her grandmother had had a lump removed from her breast before Lucie was born. For some reason, Lucie had come to associate the word with the memory of a grey cloud of mould she'd found once on the skin of a mandarin.

"I see what you mean," Gran conceded, standing up.

"What do we do?"

"Bring me the iPad," she ordered. "Let's google it."

They spent the next half an hour staring at images of rabbits with funny faces. Almost all of them had deformities far more severe than Fiver's. Lucie learnt that the condition was something called "facial nerve paralysis," which was relatively common in rabbits and often caused by an ear infection.

"Do you think that's what he had, Gran? When he was sick? An ear infection?"

"It's possible."

"Will it get better?"

"It says here that it might, with time," Gran said, before turning off the iPad. "Does it bother you?"

"Not really."

"Do you think he's ugly?"

"No!"

Pauline put an arm around Lucie's shoulders, pulled her close. "Love you."

They looked at the bunny, who had left the hutch and was dozing in a shady alcove formed by the arching branches of two silverbushes.

"You know, I was thinking before about how funny life is sometimes."

Lucie rolled onto her back, shielded her eyes from the sun. "What do you mean?"

"My stroke left me with a paralysis too."

Lucie squinted. "No, it didn't."

"It did."

"Well, I can't see it."

Pauline folded her arms across her chest like a slighted child. "Just because you can't see it doesn't mean it's not there. It doesn't feel the same."

Lucie shrugged. "So, what's funny about it?"

"Not funny ha-ha. More funny weird. Funny curious."

"Well, what's weird about it?"

Gran sighed. "Never mind."

Lucie sat up. She peered at her grandmother's face, searching for the puffy half. "Please? I want to know."

"It's just that life has a weird symmetry to it sometimes."

"Isn't it the opposite of symmetry, though?" Lucie had been learning about symmetry during home schooling. Perhaps the stroke had done more damage to Gran's brain than she'd appreciated.

"Our faces, yes. But together, Fiver and I make up a perfect whole."

"I guess . . ." Lucie still couldn't see what Pauline was talking about. Her grandmother's face looked normal. A little crumpled, perhaps, but otherwise, just the same.

"As you get older, you'll bump up against things like this. Strange connections that make you think about . . . all kinds of stuff."

Gran looked over at the rabbit, who had stopped napping and was grooming a messy patch of fur on his rump.

Lucie didn't like this talk of mysterious connections between people and animals. It scared her. She stood up. "Can I watch TV now?"

Pauline waved her away. "Go on then."

# AMY

AMY ENJOYED MASKING FOR THE SUPERMARket. It meant she didn't have to put makeup on. It meant she could stick her tongue out at the arsehole who pressed his thumb on all the avocados. She felt safer inside it, behind it. She felt shielded. Today she wore a black N95 and wandered up and down the cereal aisle, blinking against the glare of the cool white strip lights.

According to Jin, people were always having panic attacks in supermarkets. Lately, Amy could understand why. This afternoon, she hadn't brought a list with her, which meant she could be stuck in the windowless grid for over an hour, paralysed by the choices available to her.

"Amy? Amy Lee?"

It was a mother from Lucie's school.

"Britney," the woman said, placing a flat palm against her chest to introduce herself—a gesture that caused Amy to recall a Tarzan movie from her childhood. "Eloise's mother?"

Amy nodded, perhaps a little too vigorously. "How is Eloise?"

They fell into conversation—a safe, forgettable exchange. Amy had had several such encounters since the pandemic began. Parents, hungry for the daily small talk they'd lost when schools had moved online. Amy didn't understand it. She found the whole thing exhausting— not so much the conversations at the school gates but the effort of later deciphering them. As she julienned carrots for dinner, she would realise that Britney's feigned lament that Eloise was reading two years ahead of her peers and impossibly bored was actually a dig at the school for its failure to recognise her daughter's genius. When the mother-of-four member of the school council said, on seeing Amy helping out with the sausage sizzle for the first time, "I see you've got your mummy's hat on today!" she was actually both chiding Amy, in her most saccharine voice, for her prior lack of participation and guarding her own territory as the biggest contributor.

Amy would complain about it to Jin, but he would just look bored—or worse, disapproving—and that would only fan the flames of her rage even more. Instead, she held imaginary conversations in her head, in which she brutally pointed out everyone's hypocrisies to their faces. Sometimes she got herself so riled up, she had to take a couple of diazepam to calm down.

But that all changed after the accident. After the accident Amy couldn't give a shit about school, about parenting, about anything at all. Britney and the other parents sensed it. The entire ecosystem depended on people caring about what other parents thought of them. Why else would they bake the cakes and fry the sausages and volunteer at the school fete?

They were forgiving of Amy in the beginning. She was grieving, after all. She'd lost a child! They couldn't imagine! (They had imagined, of course; what parent wouldn't?) But they couldn't possibly *know*. Perhaps they understood that. There were casseroles. After a death, there are always casseroles. One parent even took a photo of the chicken cacciatore she'd made and posted it on Instagram. *Sometimes it's the little things you do that make a difference #grief.* But Amy couldn't feel outrage even about that. Her emotions were muted. It was as if she'd joined Ruby and was viewing the world from another, more evolved, dimension.

And so, during those first few months, Amy learnt that not caring was a kind of superpower. It provoked people. It upset them. Sometimes she felt so different, so alien, so removed, she wondered if she might be a psychopath. But then she read an article that said if you worried about being a psychopath, you almost certainly were not a psychopath.

Psychopath or not, Amy knew the other parents had become wary of her. She'd seen the way some of the more neurotic ones pulled their children that bit closer to them when they passed her on the street. She came to understand then that when a child dies by accident at home, rather than in a car or a hospital or at an amusement park, a question mark hovers over the parents—forever querying their vigilance, their competence, their fitness.

After a while she felt less obliterated. For better or worse, Amy could tell that her nerve endings were regenerating. Nowadays she cried. Oh, how she wept. Occasionally, she laughed. But it was different. The tears would fall, her laughter would burst out, but each time it felt like an involuntary reflex that had nothing to do with her.

The other night, while lying sleepless beside Jin—none of them were sleeping after the invasion—Amy had experienced a flashback to medical school. She was at a lecture about neuropathy and the professor was showing a slide of a Charcot foot—an appendage with no functioning sensory nerves. In the darkness, she recalled the doughy pulp formed by a thousand unnoticed knocks and bruises, and she wondered if a similar thing occurred to the anaesthetised brain. She imagined her cerebral hemispheres as a bloodied, pureed mess, and it seemed to her like a good approximation.

Britney was rattling on about how lucky she and Eloise and her husband, Tom, had been to be up north on holiday when the local lockdown had been announced. She described how their family had divided their long, semi-tropical days between home schooling and eating lunches of fresh prawns by the beach. She confessed to the guilt of seeing their friends' faces grow pale and flabby on Zoom catch-ups, while she and Tom and Eloise swam every day. Maybe, Amy thought, now would be a good time to tell Britney about the prowler. She felt she could predict Britney's reaction: first her pleasure at a new story to tell—a violent burglary in the neighbourhood, some excitement to disrupt the tedium of the endless days—at least until she remembered how close her house was to Amy's, at which point the thrill would be replaced by visceral fear. Amy was no saint. She would have told this story in a heartbeat if she'd thought it would bring her even the faintest flicker of satisfaction. But it wouldn't, she knew that, so she said nothing.

Once home, having farewelled Britney and chosen her cereal, Amy went in search of Lucie. She found her crouching beside Pauline in an overgrown corner of the backyard, watching Fiver. As Amy approached, she thought she saw the arc of not one but two pairs of rabbit haunches in the grass.

"A mirror?" she said, when she realised her mistake.

Pauline and Lucie looked up at her, and Amy was taken aback by how much her daughter resembled her mother—not in bone structure or colouring but in the formation of their expressions.

Pauline groaned as she stood up and made a half-hearted attempt to brush the green stains from her trousers. "It was Lucie's idea. But then I googled it. Turns out mirrors can be useful for single rabbits. Makes them feel less alone."

Amy looked at Fiver, sniffing his odourless reflection. It reminded her of the time Lucie had first understood the concept of mirrors. How old was she? One? One and a half? Amy had stuck a Peppa Pig sticker on Lucie's forehead, and rather than touch the mirror (as she had done countless times before), Lucie had reached for her own face. How in awe Amy had been of her daughter, even though she knew every child, sooner or later, makes this simple connection. Ruby hadn't got the chance.

Lucie stood, and Amy saw her reach for Pauline's hand. She saw the way her mother took it, instinctively, without needing to look down to see where the little fingers were in space, and she saw the way Lucie's arm had to bend just a fraction to meet the end of her grandmother's hand. She saw all these things and she was surprised by how little jealousy she felt.

The rabbit had stopped smelling the mirror and—presumably having decided that his reflection posed no threat—assumed a more relaxed posture. Pauline and Lucie cooed and made contented noises as they observed the animal, clearly pleased with their clever response to his solitude. Amy dared not interfere—their joy was too precious—but she couldn't help but think that if she were still capable of such feelings, the scene would have struck her as one of the saddest things she'd witnessed.

# PAULINE

THREE DAYS HAD PASSED SINCE THE BREAK-IN, and Pauline was still sleeping in Lucie's room. For the past two mornings, she had woken to the discovery of her granddaughter curled up beside her on the inflatable mattress. With all the stress of the home invasion, the return to face-to-face teaching, and Fiver's illness, the poor girl had started wetting the bed. Lucie was mortified and for that reason, Pauline thought it important that she remain. Now, as she lay wide-eyed and restless in the still hours of the morning, listening to her granddaughter's breathing—which sounded more like a series of heartfelt sighs—Pauline tried to remember the last time she'd shared her bed.

It must have been with Martin, a night or two before he died. Following his diagnosis, they'd begun sleeping together again. It was a couple of years after Amy had married Jin, but before the girls were born. The girlfriend was long gone. She'd packed her suitcases and fled during one of those interminable days between the surgery and the histopathology report.

Pauline worried that people would think she was fucking him because she felt sorry for him, which was not the case. If anything, she did it for selfish reasons. For the feel of another body in her bed. For the orgasms. Mostly, it was transactional. Only once or twice, towards the end, when he was too tired to return to his own apartment, had Martin stayed until morning. On those days, Pauline had made him a coffee—black with two sugars—and they had read the newspaper together in bed. She had enjoyed those mornings. They felt snug and comfortable. Like putting on an old pair of tracksuit pants, stretched in all the right places.

But that was a long time ago, long enough that she had forgotten how lovely it was to share her bed. And as she lay beside her granddaughter—who radiated warmth like a glowing coal—Pauline remembered another time, before the marriage had imploded, when she, Martin, and Amy had been holidaying in France and they'd all crammed into the same saggy double bed in whatever tiny European hotel room they had booked that summer and how thrilled she was to have them both so close—to know that Martin was not out fucking someone else and to know, from the soothing tide of her breath, that Amy was safe.

And that was why she couldn't possibly stay with Amy and Lucie and Jin any longer. At first, it was too difficult to refuse Lucie's imploring eyes, and the shattered glass and flying brick had rattled her, but if she remained here with these warm bodies and their intoxicating smells even one more day, she feared she would grow used to them, just like she had grown used to her sleeping pills after the accident. And then she would develop what the doctor called "tolerance," and she would need even more of them to get the same relief, and—perhaps worst of all—she would suffer withdrawal symptoms when she couldn't get what she craved.

# JIN

IT WAS EARLY AFTERNOON, AND JIN HAD JUST parked the car at the hospital when his phone buzzed. He stared at the text message with helpless incredulity.

*Finally got the virus. Symptoms began day before yesterday, which means you'll need to isolate. Department of Health will be in contact.*

And then, almost immediately:

*I'm fine. In case you were wondering.*

He was back in the car. Back in the same unventilated cabin in which Mindy had removed her mask and shared his air exactly four days ago. Two days before she'd developed symptoms. Smack bang at the beginning of her infectious period.

There were suddenly so many things he had to do. People he had to speak to. The consultant in charge, to let him know he wouldn't be able to come in. Amy, to tell her he would need to isolate in the granny flat for the next two weeks. The security company, who were due to come to the house later today to quote on a back-to-base alarm system. But first he had to go to the respiratory clinic at the hospital to get a PCR test.

He was not about to be caught out. He was an emergency doctor and he'd been exposed by a colleague at work. Nothing about this story was unusual. If anything, it felt a little disappointing. Because even if he couldn't admit it, least of all to himself, Jin craved a public lashing—a humiliation of epic proportions—and instead he'd received a pardon. Maybe even a reward. Because Jin didn't mind the idea of crawling inside the granny flat— the only structure he'd ever built with his own hands, the only thing, besides Lucie, he'd created that would likely outlive him—and hiding from the world.

As far as he knew, the prowler was still on the loose, and so the nights alone might be creepy, but unlike some of his friends, Jin didn't suffer from claustrophobia or cabin fever. He'd spent the first part of his childhood in tiny apartments, which had inoculated him against the kind of craving for space that afflicted so many of his peers and colleagues. He would often bite his tongue when parents from school, with the arrival of each new child, declared that they needed more space—a bigger backyard! a pool! a rumpus room!

*Can't you see*, he wanted to yell at them, *that there's a special comfort in small spaces? That we all begin life in a sac, which grows to accommodate our mass and not a centimetre more?*

Reprieved, he felt a flash of sympathy for Mindy.

*I hope its not too bad for you,* he typed. He saw he'd forgotten the apostrophe and went back to insert it before pressing send.

At once he saw three dots—pulsing like tiny stars—before they faded again.

# LUCIE

"WHAT ARE YOU DOING?!"

Lucie, who had been kneeling by the side of her bed, stood up and opened her eyes. Her mother's face—usually pallid and sickly—was flushed.

"Nothing!" she snapped, once she had got her bearings. She hid her hands behind her back.

"It didn't look like nothing," Amy said.

Lucie stared, slack-mouthed, at the mysterious being who was also her mother—a woman who walked around as if half asleep most of the time but who could still find the energy to yell at her for (of all things!) kneeling by her bed.

"So what if I was doing something? It's my room. I'm not bothering anyone."

Amy leaned against the cupboard door and slid down to the floor.

"Who taught you to"—she flicked a hand in Lucie's direction—"do *that*?"

"Nobody."

"Rubbish."

"I'm telling the truth."

"Rubbish," her mother said again, shaking her head, her unbrushed hair swirling in knotted clumps. "People don't just know how to pray. If you put a kid on a desert island when they're born, they don't happen to put their hands together one day. It's a *learned* behaviour. You learnt it from someone."

"Well, I don't remember," Lucie said and perched herself on the end of the bed because it felt awkward to be standing above her mother while she was being disciplined.

"Movies probably," Amy said. "YouTube."

Lucie's mother attributed all the world's ills to TikTok and YouTube, even though she regularly engaged with both platforms. Now she uttered the word with such disgust, it sounded like an accusation: "You *tube*," as if it were a verb to describe some aborrhent act and Lucie had just been caught doing it. How did Lucie tell her mother that if she watched anything on YouTube, it was certainly not videos of people praying?

"You know it's just outrageous," Amy said, "to think the dead go to some paradise in the sky, some endlessly accommodating place where billions of people swan around in a perpetual euphoria wearing flowing robes and golden crowns."

Lucie studied the skirting board. She didn't understand half the words her mother was saying, but she got the message. This wasn't the first conversation they'd had on the matter. But Amy wasn't finished.

"We know what's beyond the sky. Beyond the sky is the atmosphere, and beyond the atmosphere is space. And space is made up of mysterious things like black holes and nebulae and other galaxies, all of which are far more amazing and mind-blowing than anything you can read about in the Bible."

Lucie felt the need to interrupt her mother. "But what if I wasn't praying to the God from the Bible? What if I was praying to the universe? Would *that* be okay?"

"Is that what you were doing?"

Lucie looked up. In truth, when she prayed, she didn't address anyone or anything in particular. It was a series of implorations. *Please let . . . (insert plea here)*, and so she was not lying when she said, "Maybe."

Amy softened. The flush in her cheeks faded, and she looked wearied. Even her voice seemed to lose strength. "Come here," she whispered.

Hugging her mother as a ten-year-old was a very different experience from when she was a toddler. She was almost the same height as Amy, and when she leaned back, Lucie worried she might be hurting her, smothering her. Neither of them seemed to know how to fold their legs or where to put their arms. But there was comfort in feeling her mum's nose buried in her hair, warming her scalp, breathing her in.

"What do you pray for?" Amy murmured into Lucie's ear.

Lucie suspected the question was a trap. "Stuff."

Her mother didn't probe. "And does it . . . help?"

"I'm not sure," Lucie replied, because she wasn't. "Maybe."

Her mother shifted beneath her then and they fell into a softer, more comfortable arrangement. It reminded Lucie of the hugs her mum used to give a long time ago. It was like hearing a tune on the radio, which was almost but not quite the same as another equally sad song.

# AMY

AMY HAD GONE INTO LUCIE'S ROOM TO TELL her about Jin. She'd been trying to find the words to inform Lucie in the least upsetting way that none of them would be able to see or touch her dad for the next two weeks when she was confronted with the spectacle of the girl clasping her hands and moving her mouth in a silent entreaty. All the agitation and irritation Amy had been feeling since Jin had called to tell her about his exposure had erupted in a shameful burst from her untamable mouth.

Amy didn't need a psychologist to tell her she saw herself in Lucie—earnest, sensitive, vulnerable. Most of the time, she wanted to yell at her daughter to harden the fuck up, but she couldn't do that, so instead she scolded Lucie for things like praying. Amy knew this was unfair. But nobody had ever told Amy how irrational becoming a parent would make her. Instead, people had put fat books about sleep schedules and behavioural psychology into her hands as if their cool, clinical words were tools she could use when she was delirious with exhaustion and racked with anxiety about keeping her child breathing/eating/drinking/napping while trying to minimise the damage her hypervigilance was doing to the poor thing.

Nowadays it wasn't so much the sleeplessness as the challenge of being confronted by a smaller, prettier version of herself with many of the same flaws—some of which she detested so fiercely she could taste the stomach acid in the back of her mouth. Thankfully, there were other characteristics too, some from Jin and some unique to Lucie—a perfect permutation of DNA—and these were the qualities Amy loved with an alarming ferocity.

She opened the back door, eyed the granny flat. She hadn't been inside since the break-in. Jin had sorted everything out. Amy didn't know how he would sleep there, after everything that had happened, but she supposed he didn't have a choice. After the invasion, Amy felt unsafe even in the main house. The creaking floorboards and groaning pipes, once familiar sounds, now frightened her.

She would need to strip the bed and find clean sheets for Jin before he arrived home. Just the thought of doing these things was exhausting. She sat down on the top step of the back porch to gather strength. She didn't see or hear the rabbit—he was so quiet!—and so it was a surprise when she felt his furry nose against her foot.

Amy often found the sight of the rabbit heartbreaking, or, as with the case of the mirror, even a little pathetic.

But now, seeing how he was free to roam anywhere in the backyard yet chose to inhabit the small pocket of space beside her, she felt a wave of tenderness.

A couple of times, at twilight, when Amy had been searching the backyard with the aim of returning him to the hutch for the night, she and the rabbit had startled each other—he, scooting for cover, and she, letting out a shrill cry. *What kind of life is that?* Amy would think at those times. *Forever anticipating death.*

And yet now, surveying the messy yard, with Fiver by her side, Amy sensed them both grow calm. The clouds shifted and the sun showered them in buttery light. Fiver narrowed his eyes, first against the glare, and then in what looked like an attempt to doze. Amy followed suit.

As she rested, better days flashed, in orange hues, behind her lids. Days spent lying on a sandy beach, in a younger, firmer body. Days that stretched out as long and empty as the horizon, when that was not yet a terrifying thing.

# PAULINE

IF SHE HAD BELIEVED IN GOD, SHE MIGHT have thought that he or she or it was trying to make her stay. First the home invasion, and now the virus (which was really, if one thought about it, just another kind of invasion). But Pauline didn't believe in God. Instead, Pauline believed in humankind's—and particularly her own—insignificance. During her marriage to Martin, when conversations had strayed into such territory, Pauline had always maintained that events were random and any attribution of meaning or purpose to them was not just wishful thinking but a form of willful delusion.

She would offer to stay. Not for Amy—Pauline suspected her daughter had wanted her gone long ago—but for Lucie. Pauline knew the girl had a dark imagination, and who knew what horrors she would come up with on learning her father would need to quarantine for fourteen days.

Lucie was so like her mother. Watchful. Quiet. Too smart to give voice to her anxieties, which she also knew were irrational. But Pauline had a nose for such things. She knew her granddaughter had an unhealthy obsession with death. There were clues: things she said in passing, a grisly observation about how a particular animal could die, or the prospect of a missing schoolgirl she'd heard about in the news being found alive (which was apparently close to zero). Comments so ghoulish they seemed out of place on the lips of a ten-year-old child.

Pauline wasn't scared of death. When she woke up on the floor of her bathroom with a broken wrist, she had cried, not because of the pain but because she had woken up at all. And in the granny flat, when she had lain still, listening to the movements of the prowler, she'd hoped against hope that if there was a confrontation, the intruder would kill rather than maim her.

She had only ever really worried about dying for the brief period when she was the mother of a small child and the wife of a man who, at one stage at least, had seemed as if he might crumble without her. In her youth, like most young people, Pauline had felt indestructible. Death was something to be teased and taunted, unseen and remote, like a hibernating animal.

She found Amy standing at the kitchen sink. They had eaten an early dinner, and she was washing up while they waited for Jin to arrive home. There was a stack of soapy pots in front of her, but—at least for the minute Pauline was watching—all she did was gaze through the window with her wet hands softly dripping by her sides.

Pauline had a sudden urge to touch her daughter, to enfold her in her arms. But they were not the type of family to engage in such shows of affection, and so instead she said, "I can stay a little longer. Help you out. With Lucie. With everything."

# JIN

IT WAS NEARING DUSK WHEN JIN ARRIVED home. The breezeless heat and hum of wasps made it feel like summer even though it was late spring. He came through the gate in the back fence so as not to bring the virus, which he wasn't sure he was even carrying, into the main house. Lucie waved to him with sad eyes from the veranda. When he opened the door to the granny flat, he could still detect a hint of Pauline's perfume beneath the smell of whatever disinfecting product Amy had used to clean it.

He sat on the edge of the bed and fell backwards onto the mattress. His feet, still in their work shoes, remained planted on the floor. As he lay there, he admired the clean, straight lines of the ceiling he'd helped create, many months ago now, and he watched the remnants of an old spider web, caught in the breeze from the air conditioner, gently sway.

Contemplating the stretch of days that lay before him—empty but also contained—he felt only relief. Relief not to be entering the emergency department, shrouded in plastic, painfully aware of his breathing in the humid cup of the mask. Relief not to be walking inside the house only to be followed by three pairs of sorrowful eyes.

He realised he'd been waiting for this day a long time, perhaps forever, certainly since the death of Ruby. An interlude. Time to breathe. A space of his own in which to think. Yes, to think. He lifted himself onto the bed and stretched out. He felt as if he had not had sufficient time to think.

# LUCIE

SHE OPENED THE HUTCH AND PLACED THE small plate of carefully selected leaves inside the door. This evening, she'd mixed all the rabbit's favourite treats together—Tuscan kale, continental parsley, carrot tops, mint. Fiver hopped towards it, smelling the platter before pulling the kale up between his teeth.

As Fiver ate, Lucie looked towards the granny flat, which was no longer a granny flat but a daddy flat. A quarantine facility. It glowed in the muted light of dusk. She crept over to the window and peered through its new, clean, smooth glass. The bedside lamp was on and she could see the long, slim shape of her father, lying on top of the bedspread in his work clothes. His eyes were closed. Perhaps he was dead. Perhaps her father's virus-riddled body was cooling and hardening like old Play-Doh. But then she saw him wince—at a pain or at some painful image in his dream—and she knew that, at least for now, he was still alive.

Lucie had never seen a dead body. When Ruby died, she'd been at school, and it still haunted her, how she'd been sitting in math class, chewing on the end of her pencil, crushing the metallic bit around the eraser between her back molars, bored and daydreaming, while her sister was being pulled from the tepid water and given CPR, first by her father and later by the ambulance people. Nobody had told Lucie these details, of course, but she'd pieced together a story from the snippets of conversation she'd hoarded, like newspaper clippings, in her memory.

Lucie wished she'd seen her sister's body. If she'd seen her body, maybe Ruby's death would have felt like something that had happened in real life, instead of just another one of her intrusive fantasies. As it was, the only proof of her sister's death was her absence—from the high chair and the stroller and the living room rug. If Lucie had seen the body, maybe her grief would have come naturally, spontaneously, instead of feeling like one of those tedious daily tasks, like bathing and brushing her teeth, that she had to remind herself to do. And if she'd seen the body, then maybe every morning when she woke up, she would have felt the gravity of her sister's passing like a heavy stone upon her chest.

None of them had had a bath since the accident. There was a separate glass shower stall in the bathroom and they all used that. The last time they'd used the tub was when they'd filled it with ice to cool drinks at Jin's fortieth birthday party. Sometimes when her mum was locked away in her study, Lucie would lie down in its smooth ceramic bowl, so the plug made a circular dent between her shoulders, and she would look straight above her, trying to see what Ruby would have seen, if her eyes had been open in those final moments. It wasn't much. Just a white plaster sky with one bright LED light at its centre, blazing like a miniature sun.

# AMY

IT WAS ANOTHER SLEEPLESS NIGHT. AMY would have liked to blame the prowler (and indeed the incident hadn't helped; for the past three days, her body had been bracing for the shock of another exploding window), but her insomnia had begun long before the home invasion. If she had to pick a date, she would have said it arrived during the final months of her first pregnancy. In the drawer of her bedside table was a bottle of diazepam tablets, which Amy handled like expensive treats—allowing herself one (or two!) at the end of a particularly horrendous week.

She turned on the bedside lamp and pulled her laptop out from under the bed. She stacked one of Jin's pillows on top of her own, behind her head, and placed the other one on her lap. The screen was less accusing at this hour. Any words she typed now felt like stolen ones. She hadn't written anything in months, but tonight she could detect a certain ripeness about her mind.

She remembered an exercise she'd done once at a writing course. It involved breathing deeply in and out ten times and then, on the final exhalation, writing whatever came to mind. It had seemed like New Age wankery at the time, but tonight Amy was feeling open to possibilities. She inhaled and exhaled and held her fingers above the keyboard, hovering, waiting, trembling, as if it were not a computer but a Ouija board.

The word surprised her when she saw its black letters as if for the first time on the bright white screen. Amy noticed things she'd never noticed before. Its imperfect play at symmetry, for instance, how the stem of each *b* stood above the heads of the other letters, like a pair of jaunty ears.

And so, she wrote about the rabbit. She wrote about what he looked like and how he groomed himself, and the strange tidbits Lucie had been gathering like a bowerbird over the past few weeks. Most of all, however, she wrote about how—even though she had come to love him— the rabbit remained aloof and unknowable. The words, while they didn't gush, did flow more freely than they had in a long time, and the experience was invigorating in the way that good exercise can be. And it was a kind of exercise, an exercise of the mind, which explained why, when she drifted off, depleted, sometime around 3:00 AM, it was into a deep and dark and dreamless slumber.

# JIN

THE DAYS WERE LONG AND THE NIGHTS WERE terrible. Jin was still waiting on the result of his test to come back from the lab. Time was marked by the falling arc of light through the only window, text messages from Amy, and the arrival of meals and cups of tea. Jin loved it most when Lucie delivered his food. He relished her firm and rhythmic knock, followed by her (slightly forced?) smile through the glass. He would watch her bound back towards the house and wait until she'd disappeared into its depths before opening the door.

He slept during the day, like the rabbit, in brief and nervous interludes. At night he monitored the noises in the backyard—and what a cacophony it was!—for suspicious sounds. He'd always craved time to himself to think—ever since he and Amy had had kids, his mind had reverberated with their crying and complaints and pleas—but when all that turbulence was gone, the stuff that rose to the surface was the same old detritus that had been clogging up his brain for years. Rubbish planted by his parents decades before—accusations that he was hopeless, a disappointment, a failure. It was all so predictable as to be bone-achingly tedious.

To quiet his mind, Jin watched YouTube videos. Mostly instructional videos about yoga and meditation. But instead of inspiring him, the videos filled Jin with a suicidal self-loathing. An unprecedented revulsion for his sedentary, shallow-breathing self. And it was this revulsion, rather than any desire to join the yogini in her fresh-faced smugness, that prompted him to do the exercises.

As he lay on the floor and breathed deeply, suppressing annoyance at the woman's declarations that lemon water was the best way to remove toxins from the body, he spied something pale and bulky beneath the bed. He paused the video, deriving momentary satisfaction from freezing the instructor in an unflattering open-mouthed pose, and pulled the thing from its hiding place.

The bulky thing was in fact a dog-eared copy of *Watership Down*—the book Pauline and Lucie had been reading. In her haste to vacate the flat, Pauline must have left it behind. Jin wondered if she and Lucie were missing it. If they were, they hadn't made any attempt to contact him about it. Perhaps they thought it might be contaminated now.

He opened the book to a random page and held it up to his nose. Jin had always loved the smell of old pages, the mustiness, which he knew was just a mix of ink and invisible mites and the dead skin of readers, long dead themselves. He was not an avid reader, not like Amy, who, before Ruby died, had devoured novels like tasty snacks, but he did like the feeling he got when he started reading a book—the promise of it. He remembered the endorsement on Amy's book from the slightly famous author (whose titles rang a bell with people but who was not yet a household name): *This book will change your life.*

How Amy had hated that. When her excited publisher had emailed it to her, Amy had told Jin, between angry sobs, that the slightly famous author was setting her up to fail. But Jin liked the idea of a book being able to change a life. In the hours that followed Amy's outburst, he had tried and failed to recall a work of art that had moved him in that kind of seismic way.

*Watership Down* was not the sort of thing Jin ordinarily read. He usually read non-fiction written by scientists. He certainly didn't read children's books in which animals not only talked but suffered from existential crises. But perhaps it was exactly the sort of thing Jin should have been reading all these years, because several hours passed in which he didn't feel the urge to check his phone—not even once—and he only put the book down, reluctantly, when the light in the flat had faded so much that his ageing eyes could no longer make out the words.

He walked to the window and jumped up and down on the spot several times to get the blood pumping again through his muscles. Thanks to his rotations in the ICU,

Jin knew how rapidly tissues could atrophy. He often found himself impressed by both the human body's capacity for resilience and its seeming determination to die.

It was dusk. The sky was the colour of cotton candy. In the backyard, he saw the rabbit do one of those twisted leaps Lucie reliably informed him was a sign of happiness, and rather than the resentment he expected to feel at the sight of an animal relishing its (comparative) freedom, Jin experienced something else entirely. A new sensation he couldn't place. Something halfway between joy and panic. A kind of seizure of the heart.

# LUCIE

HER VISIONS—LUCIE WASN'T SURE WHAT ELSE to call them—were becoming more frequent and more violent. Up until now, her fantasies were about accidents— car crashes, falls, drownings—but ever since the prowler had put a brick through the window, the images had taken a darker turn. Mostly she saw heads smashed in—with bricks, of course, but also shovels and clubs, things lying around the backyard from the suspended renovation, slabs of timber, broken tiles, PVC piping.

She'd liked it better when Gran was living in the flat. Everybody had seemed happier then. Her mum had still had her privacy, which Lucie knew she needed desperately. Gran had still had her own bathroom. Her dad had been around—not much, he was never around much— and Lucie had still seen him occasionally.

Now, when Lucie was not at school, she spent as much time as she could outside, where she was able to breathe a little easier. She read (mostly comics because Gran's copy of *Watership Down* had gone missing), wrote in her journal, played with Fiver. But even the rabbit seemed more tense than usual. He had started digging holes in the backyard, and Lucie wondered if he was creating his own burrow or if—like a prisoner in a cartoon—he was trying to dig his way out. She knew from her research that it was the female rabbits, rather than the bucks, who dug the burrows. Lucie wondered if Fiver could sense what was happening to the human beings around him.

She longed to have the senses of an animal. Perhaps then she might have a warning when something bad was about to happen. If she had a warning, she could prepare herself. She could run away. She could hide.

# PAULINE

A CHANGE HAD DESCENDED UPON THE HOUSE that evening, perhaps the whole neighbourhood. God knew the wind had a nasty bite to it as Pauline walked the streets. But it was better than stewing in the charged atmosphere at home. She pulled her jacket tighter around her shoulders, jerked violently on the zip. A large moon was beaming, and she remembered how Jin had told her about a couple of nurses in the emergency department who were so convinced of the full moon's mind-altering powers they kept a lunar calendar in the tearoom.

And maybe that was the cause: human beings responding to some weird gravitational energy. Up until this point, Pauline had blamed the unease on three generations of women jammed into the same space. As she walked, it occurred to her that if Lucie were a little bit older and Pauline were a lot younger, they would all be menstruating together. At the mercy of yet another invisible force.

As it was, sharing a bathroom was hard enough. Nobody mentioned the accident. They didn't have to—the bath was there, large and white, dominating the space and demanding attention. Instead, they were painfully polite. There was no lock on the door, and there had been quite a few awkward moments, followed by a rush of embarrassed apologies. Pauline had even once glimpsed her daughter's naked form through the glass walls of the shower. How beautiful her skin was. Opalescent.

Pauline had spent much of Amy's childhood worrying about strangers wanting to possess her daughter. Perhaps it was from that place, a place of protectiveness, that she had said what she had said the night before Amy's wedding. When she'd asked her daughter (how she cringed at the memory!) whether she thought Jin would ever be able to truly satisfy her. Amy, of course, had thought Pauline's words were racist—some clumsy and roundabout reference to his penis—but Pauline hadn't meant it that way. She would have said the same thing to Amy no matter whom she was marrying. Her daughter had always seemed not quite of this world—too smart, too sad, too special—but then perhaps all mothers felt this way about their children.

It was different with Lucie—the space of a generation allowed them to truly see and hear each other. Every so often Lucie would do something that reminded her unexpectedly of Jin, and that was when Pauline felt both the most distanced from, and the most in love with, her only granddaughter. Even then, it was possible to grow tired of the girl. Her young brain never stopped, and her questions were endless. At these times, Pauline would grab her jacket from the hat stand in the hallway and declare that she was going for a walk.

As she strolled, Pauline looked in through the windows of the Californian bungalows and Victorian terraces she passed. She recalled the children's paintings of rainbows that had once been taped to the glass, the chalk drawings on the footpaths with sunny messages like *Have a good day*. Where were these bright offerings now? Instead, the windows revealed men and women resigned to a new way of living, bent over softly illuminated desks.

She soon found herself at "the house with the letterbox." The owners, whom Pauline had never met, were renowned in the neighbourhood for the miniature scenes they would create inside the inbuilt display window of their letterbox. Elves for Christmas. Maple leaves for autumn. Seashells for summer. The home had become an essential place to stop during her afternoon strolls with Lucie and Ruby, before the accident. But this evening the letterbox didn't bring any joy to Pauline. If anything, it depressed her. Although spring was nearly over, the letterbox was still stuck in winter. A miniature snowman lay on its side on a mound of limp cotton wool, no longer white but a sad ash colour.

Tired now, Pauline leaned against the fence to gather breath and strength. She didn't see the key ring but heard the tinkle of the chain as she nudged it with her foot. She bent down to pick it up. It was dyed a ridiculous shade of purple, but its form was unmistakable: a rabbit's foot.

Lucie would be horrified—horrified to know that such a thing existed, that her grandmother had touched it. But Pauline supposed it must belong to someone; perhaps it was a gift from a loved one, or a lucky charm—and so, rather than dropping it back on the ground or throwing it in a nearby rubbish bin, she hung it by its metal ring from the top of one of the palings. The purple shone against the white backdrop of the picket fence, impossible to miss.

As she turned to head home, bracing against the wind and tucking her cold and throbbing head into the flimsy hood of her jacket, Pauline marvelled at the strangeness of human beings who would attach the amputated limb of a small prey animal to a key chain for good luck. And yet, walking back past the bowed heads of the men and women hard at work inside their houses, behind fences prowlers could easily jump and windows burglars could easily break, she felt that perhaps she did appreciate some of the appeal after all.

# JIN

IT WAS NEARING MIDNIGHT. THE MAIN HOUSE was dark. Jin turned off the lamp and begrudgingly climbed into bed. He was not tired. He observed a routine because he didn't know what else to do. Sometimes he imagined himself as an astronaut, suspended in space and sealed off from the universe.

He was about to open a mindfulness app on his phone (more for the company of another voice than for the meditative practice itself) when he heard the noise. In the past five days Jin had become familiar with the flatulent growls of the possums, the mewls of the neighbourhood cats, and Fiver's thumps against the walls of the hutch, but this sound was different. This sound was bold, heavy, human.

Jin's response was immediate. He grabbed the mop Amy had left in the bathroom and burst through the door. He stood on the front step of the flat, wielding his weapon, a bare-chested warrior in the moonlight.

There were so many places for a person to hide: behind the shed, crouched in the silverbush, wedged in the crevice between the fence and the wall of the granny flat. Jin searched them all. He used his phone as a flashlight and the mop as a walking stick, but—apart from a dead pigeon beside the compost heap—there was nothing to find.

He was jumping at shadows. An effect of the break-in. He probably should have been embarrassed, but he was not. In fact, when Jin returned to the flat and collapsed into bed a few minutes later, he felt calmer than he had in days. When it mattered, when his family was in danger, he hadn't hesitated to protect them. For the first time that week, Jin fell into a restful sleep.

# AMY

SOMEHOW, THE ANNIVERSARY ALWAYS CAUGHT
Amy by surprise. She would feel a building simmer of
agitation until, inevitably, it bubbled over, scalding
whoever happened to be closest (usually Lucie). In
the ensuing stunned silence, Amy would experience a
sudden clarity of thought—about dates and cycles and
anniversaries and their interplay with grief—and she
would be seized, not so much with guilt (though there
was that) but with a profound sense of betrayal. As if her
body and mind had conspired against her.

Today, however, she couldn't claim ignorance. As soon
as she'd opened her laptop that morning, the date had
reverberated in her brain. The weather was so uncannily reminiscent of that awful day, Amy suspected its
significance would have dawned on her anyway. In past
years—there were three before this one—it had always
been cooler, warmer, wetter, more overcast. But this year
there was the same smattering of clouds and the very

same—almost celestial—light, which rather than simply illuminating things seemed to make them glow from within. Anybody else would have declared it a perfect late spring day.

All this, Amy knew, was playing on her nerves. Her skin now buzzed with a faint prickle of electricity. She felt the pull of something again. A want. Never mind that what she craved was destruction. A reckoning. A massive motherfucking fight.

# PAULINE

IT ARRIVED THAT AFTERNOON, ON THE POW-
dery wings of a moth.

"Nai Nai says moths are the dead coming back to visit us."

Time slowed and Pauline had the unshakeable sensation of not being in control of her speech or her movements—of being carried towards some preordained
destination in small but unstoppable increments.

"That's nonsense," Amy said, without looking up from
her laptop. She was seated on a stool in the kitchen,
while Pauline and Lucie sat at opposite ends of the dining table.

Pauline pretended to concentrate on her already-
completed sudoku puzzle.

"Not only moths. Birds too. Things that fly," Lucie
went on.

"It's a nice idea, hon," Pauline said, her voice hushed
and—she hoped!—expressing her desire for the conversation to end.

Amy closed her laptop with a metallic snap, which made Lucie jump a little. "That insect," she said, standing up and pointing towards the curtains where the moth was cowering, "is *not* your sister. That moth is not Ruby."

The sudoku grid swam before Pauline's eyes. She was at war with herself, and when the words arrived, they exploded from her lips in reluctant, spittle-laden bursts. "For fuck's sake, Amy, just let the girl believe in something."

Amy's attention shifted from daughter to mother. Lucie, like any prey animal, snatched her opportunity to escape.

"What are you afraid of anyway?" Pauline hissed when the girl was gone.

Amy's spine straightened, and her already-long neck lengthened. "Are you seriously going to lecture me, *today*, of all days?"

Pauline looked down at her puzzle, at its neat boxes and orderly numbers. "You don't have a monopoly on grief, Amy. We're all grieving. Today. Every day." She paused to suck in more air. She'd forgotten how much exertion was involved in arguing. She was not the same woman, the same mother, she once was. "Besides, I'm curious. So what if Lucie thinks her dead sister has come back as a moth? What are you so afraid of? Sentimentality?"

"Sentimentality," Amy said, gravely, and without a hint of irony, "is death itself."

"In books maybe. But what use is childhood if not for magic and imagination and sentimentality? She's a child, Amy. A child!"

"And I'm a mother!" Amy roared.

"As am I."

Amy took her time, enjoying it, savouring it, speaking almost unnaturally slowly and enunciating every syllable. "But you're also the kind of mother who gets out of stroke rehab and decides that instead of supporting her grieving daughter, she should go on a fucking cruise."

And Pauline didn't have an answer to that. She walked out.

# JIN

THE LAB HAD LOST JIN'S SWAB AND IN SO doing had erased him from the world. "I'm sorry but I have no record of you. That name does not exist." It struck Jin—who'd felt invisible ever since taking up residence in the granny flat (perhaps longer, perhaps forever)—that the default position nowadays was one of non-existence. All events had to be proved through the provision of numbers and images and documents. Never mind that as Jin spoke to the bored lab administrator on the phone, he could feel his body displacing the air, his head flattening the pillow, his legs indenting the mattress. Never mind that he had a clear memory of not only the feel of the plastic stick probing the deep recesses of his nasopharynx but the somewhat disturbing sight of blood on the tissue when he'd blown his nose the following day.

Jin recalled how, for months after Amy's dad had died, the telephone company had continued to send increasingly bold and colourful—yellow, orange, and then red—bills for his mobile phone. In that situation, by contrast, it was Martin's non-existence that had required proof, which made Jin wonder whether part of what everyone was seeking by amassing these accounts and subscriptions to mobile phones and streaming services was a kind of perverted legacy. A posthumous reminder to friends and family that they'd once occupied space in the digital universe too, that not so long ago they had texted and binged with the best of them. And perhaps it was a lack of such records that led to Ruby being so easily and promptly forgotten, not by them (never!) but by the wider world. Apart from the letter from the maternal-child health nurse recalling Ruby for her twelve-month immunisations—a document Jin had thankfully destroyed before it got to Amy but not before it had caused him to rush to the bathroom in a paroxysm of violent sobs he later pretended was a bout of food poisoning—no administrators ever came looking for her.

And so, without the results, without knowing whether the virus was replicating inside his body, Jin persisted in a kind of purgatory. And yet he didn't feel uncertain. Last night he'd suffered a chill unlike any he'd ever experienced. He'd wondered whether the creeping electric sensation bore any resemblance to formication—a phenomenon that had occupied Jin's imagination ever since he'd first heard about it in medical school. As the night wore on, he'd felt increasingly sure that the experience was caused by the virus hooking its spike proteins onto his cells.

Unfortunately, a vibe was not enough. He needed a diagnosis. He would have to drive back to the hospital tomorrow morning and have another test. But he didn't feel as if he could manage it. Over the years he'd heard his GP friends express bewilderment at patients who declared they were "too sick to come in." *Who was too sick to see a doctor?* they would ask, amused at the irony, at the comical double bind. And yet now Jin felt that this was exactly the level of catch-22 incapacitation he was suffering.

When Ruby died, he'd taken two weeks. Two measly weeks of bereavement leave. Everybody had said it wouldn't be enough. But how did one estimate what would be enough? Almost half a decade had elapsed since Ruby's death, and Jin still carried the deep well of emptiness around with him everywhere he went. Allocation of sick leave was not something he'd ever been taught during medical school. It was one of those skills, like taking blood and inserting peripheral lines and writing on drug charts and breaking bad news and dealing with bereaved, angry, psychotic, intoxicated, demented, and delirious patients, that interns were expected to pick up on the job.

Some estimates of healing were straightforward: six weeks for a fractured bone, two weeks for a soft-tissue injury, five days for a wound on the face, ten for an equivalent wound on the back, chest, limbs. Jin regurgitated these figures when asked but remained sceptical of the body's ability to repair itself in neat round numbers.

Jin also knew that scar tissue was never quite as strong as the original. Depending on its location, it was more prone to rupture, infection, degeneration. Sometimes the scars themselves led to new problems—contractures, obstructions of the bowel or the fallopian tubes. In the case of keloids, the skin didn't know when to stop forming scar tissue. It grew thicker and more gnarled in response to the mere memory of trauma.

And nowadays memories were everywhere. Everybody carried little shiny memory grenades in their pockets. Jin might be lying on his bed reading the newspaper on his phone, totally unsuspecting, and with as little as a beep from his device, he could be distracted by a photo montage with an unimaginative title like "On This Day Five Years Ago" or "By the Sea" or "Springtime," set to Muzak. In the thick of his rage at Steve Jobs and technology and artificial intelligence, he would feel a wave of exactly the kind of melancholic nostalgia the montage had been designed to elicit, and his anger would be supplanted by a profound, almost nihilistic, disappointment—at society and at his life and most of all at himself.

# LUCIE

LUCIE DID WHAT SHE ALWAYS DID DURING AN argument: she hid. She had worked out that she was one of those kids—there were a handful of them in her class—who could disappear. She was neither Asian nor white. She was neither blonde nor raven-haired. She was neither fat nor thin, tall nor short, beautiful nor ugly. She was a mousy-brown brunette who, according to her mum, was tracking almost exactly along the fiftieth centile for weight and height. She was wholly unremarkable, remarkably so. The extraordinary things about her were invisible—her memory, her vocabulary, her appetite for the macabre.

For the most part, this invisibility suited Lucie just fine. She felt grateful she wasn't Jenny with the terrible eczema, who slapped her itching cheeks (instead of tearing them apart with her fingernails); or Marlo with the warts like fleshy buttons all over his hands; or Pippa with the birthmark that looked like someone had splashed a glass of red wine in her face.

Lucie had preferred home schooling. She didn't have to spend recess walking the perimeter of the playground, alone. Being smart and keen to get distasteful things out of the way, she could finish her tasks halfway through the day and spend the rest of her time reading, drawing, watching TV, and lying around, which was what she was doing now, in a patch of long weeds in the backyard.

Over time, Lucie had learnt that if she hunted Fiver down with outstretched fingers, he would always reject her advances, but if she lay still and waited, his curiosity would almost always get the better of him, and soon enough she would feel his nose—dry and furry and so unlike a dog's slimy snout—nudging her thigh, shoulder, foot, hand, cheek.

Lucie loved how the rabbit was different from human beings in this regard. Now that she was back at school, she spent her lunchtimes imploring the universe to conjure up some company for her. Someone to complain to about her boring lunchbox of salami sandwiches and soggy strawberries. Someone to gossip and giggle with about the ridiculously long fart Jayden had let rip in art class. But nobody ever came. Not even Sahara, who had kind eyes and would occasionally make a pair with Lucie for games during PE (without any obvious dismay) when her best friend was away.

Human beings, it seemed to Lucie, lacked curiosity about the world. A curiosity that rabbits had in endless supply. Today, for instance, the longer Lucie lay in the grass, the more still she remained, the braver and more brazen Fiver became. And so Lucie, delighted, lingered in the weeds, imitating death in order to feel Fiver probing her contours, sniffing her, licking her, contemplating her, if only for a few precious moments more.

# AMY

AMY SHOULDN'T HAVE SAID THE WORDS, BUT she couldn't hold them in any longer. In truth, they were the same words she had wanted to yell when Pauline went on her trip all those years ago. It took saying them for Amy to realise that every conversation since had been a failed attempt to confront her mother.

Pauline, true to habit, had stormed off to the backyard. Now Amy was alone, perched on a stool in the kitchen. Her laptop was open, but she couldn't work on the novel. It was too quiet. What had become of all the birdsong? Were the magpies and mynahs horrified by her lack of filial piety too? She suddenly missed Jin with an intensity that was unfamiliar to her. Not that Jin would have intervened in any meaningful way—he often appeared terrified of her mother—but he would have been another pair of eyes, another witness, and that alone would have given Amy strength.

Unsure how to occupy this strange and soundless aftermath, Amy got up to fill the kettle. As the water somersaulted within its metal chamber, she gazed through the window into the backyard. She had a partial view of her daughter through the blades of the long grass, and every now and then she spotted the arc of the rabbit's back—a thread of gold amidst the green.

The kettle's hiss obscured the sound of her mother's slippered feet on the tiled floor, which meant Pauline was right behind her—looking more withered than ever—when Amy turned away from the window to fetch a tea bag from the pantry.

"Making tea?"

Why, when a situation demanded honesty, did people of a certain class—people like her and her mother—insist on brewing hot drinks and hiding behind their civility?

"You want a cup?"

"If it's not too much trouble."

Amy opened the cupboard next to the sink to retrieve another mug. She chose the red one with a heart-shaped chip on the rim. She poured hot water onto the tea bag and watched the liquid slowly darken. The steam whirled and eddied around her. It was now or never.

"Mum, I need to ask you something."

"Ask away."

"Why . . ." Amy didn't want it to sound like an accusation, so she kept her voice low, almost a whisper. "Why were you bathing her? At that time of day?"

After a long pause, Pauline spoke. "I'd made custard."

Amy remembered the dirty dishes in the sink—they had sat, untouched, for days. Later, she had scrubbed the white substance stuck to the bottom of the pan without turning a thought to what food it had once been.

"She had it all over her hair and hands and face."

Amy gripped the kitchen counter for support. She felt as if she might faint.

"There are lots of us, you know."

Amy jiggled the tea bags. "Us?" She was angry now, and the anger gave her strength.

"Zombies. The bereaved."

She could have said something, cut her mother to shreds, but she was curious. She dumped the tea bags in the sink and placed the mugs on the kitchen counter.

For the next minute Amy watched Pauline trace the rim of the mug with the index finger of her left hand, its otherwise circular orbit interrupted by the heart-shaped dip. She noticed for the first time that the last joint of her mother's finger was marked with a Heberden's node—a telltale sign of osteoarthritis. Pauline was an old woman. Sometimes Amy forgot this.

"Those weeks in the hospital after the stroke were some of the loneliest of my life," Pauline began. "I never saw a consultant, not once." She looked down at her cast, frayed and grey at the edges. "But I'm not complaining. And it's not as if I was alone. I was surrounded by nurses and physiotherapists and social workers." She took a sip of her tea. "I suppose what I'm trying to say is that even with all the noise and activity around me, or perhaps because of it, I still felt hopelessly alone. More hopelessly alone, even, than when I left your father."

The muscles in Amy's neck and shoulders tightened. As usual, her instincts had been off. There was no mounting confession here, only more of the same *woe is me*.

"You see, when your father and I separated, I had *hate* to keep me company. And the hate was a kind of energy. But when Ruby died, there was nobody to hate. Except myself. And my body. Which I did. Believe me. But what can you do with self-loathing when you're bound to a hospital bed, always surveilled and barely able to move, banned even from eating or drinking without the supervision of a speech pathologist? You certainly can't do what you want to do, which is to destroy yourself." Tears were streaming down her mother's elongated cheeks. "And so I lay there, with my eyes closed, replaying one scene on an endless loop. The scene of me on the tiled floor of your bathroom, flailing like a fish. Helpless to do anything but wait. And hope."

# PAULINE

ONCE SHE HAD STARTED, SHE COULDN'T STOP. It was as if an obstruction somewhere deep inside Pauline's brain had dissolved and her cerebral juices, stagnant for so long, were free to flow again. And so she told Amy how, one night during her hospital stay, a nurse had found her in the bathroom slamming her head against the wall and how the nurse had notified a timid-looking doctor, who had referred Pauline to the "consultant liaison psychiatry team." And she told her daughter how the following day a member from the consultant liaison psychiatry team had asked her whether she wanted to kill herself, and when she had replied, "Yes, desperately," he had commenced her on an antidepressant, something beginning with *e*.

And she told Amy how the antidepressant had taken away all her feelings—good and bad—and all her motivations—suicidal and otherwise—and how, months later, in rehab, she'd met a woman in her seventies who had spoken non-stop about her cruise-ship holidays, and Pauline had realised as she listened to the retiree that a cruise was perhaps the only legitimate way for a person (and particularly a woman) in her situation to escape her life. Which was exactly what she wanted to do. Escape. And punish herself. And as someone who had, not so long ago, prided herself on independent travel to cultural destinations and looked down on package tourists with their loud shirts and bum bags, Pauline knew that two weeks on a cruise ship would deliver exactly what she was seeking: escape and punishment, perhaps in equal measure.

And she told Amy how at first it really was excruciating. The relentless noise—excited chatter and background Muzak and foreground cover bands. The lights—fairy ones around the pool, chandeliers in the dining room, flashing disco balls on the dance floor. But after a while she had fallen into conversation with the people wearing the loud shirts and the bum bags, and she was shocked to discover that some (most!) of them were wittier and more grounded than many of the snooty so-called friends she'd collected like pretty shells from school councils and philanthropic boards over the years.

And she told Amy how rather than feeling grateful for having shared a couple of meaningful exchanges with these relative strangers, she had instead felt terribly sad. Sad that she had wasted so much of her life wearing strained smiles around people she really didn't like very much, people who—if she was honest—*disgusted* her.

And she told Amy how in that instant she had missed them—Amy, Jin, Lucie, and Ruby—with an ache as profound and agonising as labour pains, only without the promise of any relief, or respite, or a child.

# JIN

THE CHEST PAIN WAS BACK. JIN HAD JUST FIN-
ished eating the lukewarm lasagne Lucie had delivered
for dinner when it seized him. Only this time it felt like
the real thing. He was clawing at his throat in the same
way his father had done when he had his heart attack,
aged forty-three. *If I survive this*, Jin vowed, *I'll spend
more time with him.*

Even before the pain had reached its peak, Jin's mind
was already twenty steps ahead: he was in the frenzied
emergency department, looking up at the furrowed face
of the cardiologist on call (most likely Terry Lam or
Kelly Kaur); he was being whisked into the cath lab with
its plank-like bed and giant screens projecting the tortu-
ous outline of his coronary arteries for all to see.

In some ways this scenario was worse than death—to
have his colleagues gathered around him like mourners
around a coffin, their faces obscured by N95 masks so he
would never know whether they were feeling smug that

it had happened to him and not them, or terrified that it would be one of them next.

He tried to breathe but the air was as thick as honey and the gasping and moaning, when they began, seemed to come from somebody else. He'd had this sensation while dreaming—of wanting desperately to scream but being unable to, of being starved of the necessary air.

He called Amy, who seemed to pick up on the panic in his voice. She told him to take an aspirin from the box of medicines in the bathroom before she hung up to call for an ambulance. A few minutes later he received a text.

*I said you're isolating and to come through the back.*

He replied using the emoji of two hands clasped in prayer, which could mean "thank you" or "thank God" or I'm praying for the best.

The last time he'd called an ambulance was for Ruby, and now his thoughts turned to her, to his baby girl, to her tiny nasal passages and her delicate airways with their frond-like cilia filling with bathwater. He envisaged the spongy tissues of her lungs sucking in fluid as if it were a life source, like breast milk, instead of what it actually was: a tasteless, colourless poison. And that was where Jin's thoughts remained, snagged on this devastating image, when he heard the wail of the ambulance siren.

# LUCIE

LUCIE HAD GROWN USED TO HEARING SIRENS.
Ambulances were some of the only vehicles allowed to
roam the streets unchecked during the worst days of the
pandemic. But those sirens were a distant background
noise, one that might prompt nothing more than a brief
intrusive thought. This sound was something else. It
didn't wax and wane but was a blanket of noise, a blare
that obliterated everything else. Until it didn't. And in
the proceeding silence Lucie heard a knock coming from
the gate in the back fence.

She peered through a gap in the timber to see two people in matching navy uniforms and orange duck-billed
masks.

"Hi there," one of them said to what Lucie assumed
was a sliver of her face through the fence. "Your mum
called us. Can you open up?"

When Lucie would later remember the scene, it would
feel like a clip from a movie. The stroboscopic effect of the

ambulance lights probably had a lot to do with it. Here: her father's masked face bathed in rosy light. There: her mother's knotted brow in a pool of oceanic blue.

Lucie hadn't been home when the ambulance was called for Ruby, but she'd imagined it countless times—a panicked scene with people shouting and wailing and weeping. But today, she was struck by how calm and organised everything was. Her dad wasn't strapped to a stretcher with a white sheet wrapped tight around his body. Instead, he stepped up and into the bright interior of the ambulance as if he were casually entering a room in a house.

Relatives weren't allowed in the ambulance or the hospital because of the COVID restrictions. Lucie, Amy, and Pauline had no choice but to wave helplessly from the gate in the back fence. As the paramedics closed the double doors behind her father, Lucie remembered the times before Ruby was born when he would go on one of his conferences and return a few days later, looking tired but also happier, standing at the front door with a suitcase full of dirty clothes and a couple of gifts from the airport that none of them needed.

• • • • • • • • •

The rabbit froze. His options were to hide or freeze, but the lights and sounds were coming from everywhere at once and he didn't know where to go. He remained frozen when the mosquito net was whisked away to reveal the pale sphere of the moon, and he remained frozen when the door to the hutch rattled open. He even remained frozen when the pair of cool but slightly clammy hands scooped him up and set him down upon the dewy grass.

• • • • • • • • •

# AMY

IT FELT WRONG TO BE AT HOME WHILE JIN
was in the hospital. If they couldn't be with him, at least
let them be in that terrible, timeless space of the emergency waiting room. Let them be drinking their vending
machine coffees and bearing witness to the pain of all
the people loitering in various states of sleep and prostra-
tion, their faces buried in pillows made from rolled-up
jackets, oversized backpacks, the curve of shoulders, the
flesh of bellies.

It didn't feel right for them to be where they were,
in their pyjamas, in their warm beds, as he was being
hooked up to machines and pierced with needles. It was
too easy for them to forget—or if not to forget, then at
least to pretend that none of it was happening. If Jin was
dying, Amy wanted to feel it. If something bad was happening, she wanted to be present for it.

Amy had worked out from the resuscitation times
recorded in Ruby's hospital file (which she had requested

under the Freedom of Information Act) that while her daughter was dying, she had been in the final stages of an event at a writers festival in Adelaide. She had been speaking about her book—the short story collection she'd been working on for a decade, which would in the following months go on to sell just shy of six hundred copies—and while she could never know for sure, Amy felt certain in the way one can feel certain about such things that Ruby's heart had stopped beating at the exact moment when Amy had dropped the erudite quote she'd rehearsed ad nauseam in the musty hotel room, perfecting its delivery to look casual and spontaneous. And she also felt certain that as Jin had sealed his hot mouth on the cold, wet lips of their baby daughter, her own body, 726 kilometres away, was growing taller and broader with each awed sigh from the audience, as if her admirers were breathing life into her.

Hours later, as Amy sat, pale and tearless, waiting for her plane to board, random people on Twitter tagged her in photos from the event, and she couldn't help but feel a revulsion at her pink cheeks and puffy chest—at the *excessiveness* of her existence.

She hadn't known, of course. How could she have possibly known? For her to have known, some supernatural powers of telepathy would have had to descend on her, and every person of sound mind knew that such phenomena were not real. These were the sorts of things Amy's friends said to comfort her in her guilt.

She was completely oblivious, drunk on vanity, signing books, when Jin rang her. By then, Ruby was tucked away in the back of an ambulance with two paramedics taking turns to do the work her heart refused to do. At first Amy didn't believe him. Her husband's wavering voice didn't sound like someone playing a prank, but how could what he was saying possibly be true? Surely this was just some nightmare summoned up out of Amy's internalised misogyny? A mother punished in the most horrific way for daring to leave her family.

And yet it was true. In her pain and shock and grief and disbelief, Amy had the thought (which she would never admit to anyone, not even to the most disarming therapist in the most probing session): *Why couldn't this have happened to him?* Why was he able to go away, sometimes for weeks at a time, and return to a house that looked exactly the same as when he had left it, perhaps neater even, with bright windows and a swept veranda, and a family who greeted him, their hearts not only vigorously beating but leaping a little at the sight of him?

And so it was that Amy, the mother, became one of the last people to know. After the father and the sister and the grandmother. But also after the emergency operator, after the paramedics, and—worst of all—after the nosy neighbours who'd heard the approaching sirens and peered with perverse excitement between the thick blades of their plantation shutters.

She could not be the last to know again. As awful as it might be, she would rather see the pain etched into Jin's face, the slow greying of his cheeks and lips, the hungered Cheyne-Stokes breathing, than let her imagination have its way with his death.

She stared at the ceiling. She remembered a night not long before Ruby's death when the whole family climbed into bed together. Jin must have been on leave because he wasn't distracted by work and was feeling playful. It was his idea to get the flashlight out. Oh, how Lucie had loved it. Even Ruby, who had recently started giggling in that delightful way small babies have, was laughing at the scary illuminated faces Jin was making in the blue cave formed by their blanket. And when they felt suffocated by that dark and tiny space, they threw the covers off with the gusto of creatures shedding old skins, and Jin made shadow puppets with his hands across the bedroom wall. A man with a knobbly forehead. A turtle with a long neck. Rabbits. Lot and lots of rabbits. Amy remembered they loved the rabbits most of all.

# PAULINE

PAULINE THOUGHT OF JIN, ALONE IN THE HOS-
pital, and her thoughts turned, as all thoughts inevitably
do, to herself. She remembered her first trip to the emergency department in the back of an ambulance. Like Jin,
she had been alone—not because health orders or the
hospital had dictated it but because (perhaps worse!)
there was nobody to accompany her. Her ex-husband
was dead, her daughter was traveling, and her son-in-law
was picking up one granddaughter from school to race
to the children's hospital where her other granddaughter lay, cold and blue and wet, waiting for someone to
certify her.

Four years ago, the doctors were unmasked and there
was no social distancing. In fact, Pauline remembered
one male nurse who was such a close talker—shouting as
if the real reason Pauline wasn't responding was that she
couldn't hear him, rather than that a clot had momentar-
ily disrupted the blood supply to a small but significant

part of her brain—that she felt the fine spray of his spittle all over the feeling part of her face.

Now, sometime after 2:00 AM, she crept out of the house and strolled to the nearby all-night store. Pauline hadn't smoked in decades, and so she wasn't accustomed to the plain paper on the box. She was taken aback by the warning and the accompanying image of a red and purple necrotic mouth. Who knew cancer could be so colourful? But once she was outside with the cool air on her face, she remembered what Jin had once said: No point controlling the octogenarian's sugars to prevent diabetic eye disease in ten years' time. Let him have the lemon slice!

Besides, smoking made her feel young again. When Pauline smoked, she had smooth skin and perfect breasts, and she was waiting behind the shed for Alex Patton to stick his tongue down her throat and thrust his fingers inside her underwear. She had not yet met Martin or been in love (with all the terrible heartache that accompanied being in love). Her heart was strong, ox-like, and her womb was small and tight as a fist.

As she smoked, she wondered what would happen if Jin died. It would be near impossible for any of them to recover from the blow. *And then there were three.* One woman for each generation. And Pauline among them. *How is that fair?* Which, of course, was what Amy and Lucie would be thinking whenever they looked at her. Every glance loaded with the same question: *Why are you still here?*

It was nearing 3:00 AM. During her thirty-minute walk, Pauline had encountered only two other human beings: a young woman with melancholic eyes walking her Pomeranian, and a middle-aged man with a tattoo on his face who, on passing Pauline, muttered something about how everything in life was a lie. As far as she knew, the prowler was still on the loose, but she wasn't scared. All the talking had eviscerated her. She felt like a husk of a person.

When she arrived home, she sneaked through the gate in the back fence, which announced her arrival with a squeak. A brown mouse darted across the grass and disappeared into the granny flat. In all the excitement of his departure, Jin must have forgotten to close the door. Pauline peered into the room that had been her home until the break-in. How quickly, she thought, a space morphed to accommodate its new resident. Now, where her quilt had once been pulled tight and neat across the mattress, a brown bedspread lay in a large, dark, muscular mass.

Pauline scared the mouse away before pulling the door to the flat closed. On her way back to the house, almost as an afterthought, she peered inside the hutch. She looked for a flash of fur, the glisten of an eye, but there was nothing. She realised that the door to the hutch, like the door to the granny flat, was ajar. She did a cursory search of the backyard but she knew, even as she looked beneath the silverbush and behind the shed, that the rabbit was gone.

# JIN

THERE WAS NO TERRY LAM OR KELLY KAUR.
There was no cardiac cath lab. Jin's electrocardiograph
and cardiac enzymes were normal. Even a quick echocar-
diogram done by Jin's boss, the head of the emergency
department, revealed a beautiful and flawless heart. He
didn't have COVID either. His new PCR had come back
negative.

Now, as Jin waited for the nurse—a young woman
called Chloe from the UK whom he'd worked with a
couple of times—to remove the drip from his arm, he felt
as if his body was gaslighting him. And while the imagined scenes in the cath lab had filled him with despair,
this reality now felt like a far worse fate. Jin knew that,
for all their performed deference to mental health, his
colleagues (many of whom were pathologically anxious
themselves) still viewed anxiety as a weakness. He'd seen
the subtle but unmistakable change in his boss's face

when his heart offered a normal echo. A coldness of the eyes. A stiffening of the jaw.

The emergency resident had made an appointment for Jin with one of the consultant psychiatrists—a professor with a long Sri Lankan surname everybody struggled to pronounce—in two weeks' time. Jin knew he must have bumped someone else off the list to get an appointment so soon, and this only exacerbated his guilt.

As Chloe bent down to remove the cannula from his arm, he caught a whiff of her perfume and a glimpse of her bra through the neck of her scrubs. He would have to tell Amy about Mindy. He knew it as he took off the hospital gown and got back into the clothes he'd been wearing when the ambulance arrived. He knew it as he walked past the gift shop in the hospital foyer with its silver *Get well soon* balloons and velveteen stuffed toy rabbits. (Why was it always rabbits? Didn't people know that rabbits don't love you back?) And he knew it as he travelled down in the lift to the hospital carpark, where he'd arranged for Amy to pick him up. He knew it and yet his heart still lurched as he opened the passenger door.

"It's not your heart then," Amy said when he'd sat down. She was parked uncannily close to where Jin had pulled over the day, less than two weeks ago, that Mindy had intercepted his car. Rather than unnerve him, this coincidence only strengthened Jin's resolve to confess. It was as if the universe his mother inhabited—the one in which everything was imbued with meaning, where numbers and even the arrangement of objects could determine a person's fate—had been revealed to him.

"Not my heart but my brain."

"Did they organise any follow-up?"

"With a psych."

Amy stared straight ahead with her hands on the wheel. Jin wanted to reach out to her, put his hand on her leg, bury his head in her lap, before everything changed.

"I need to tell you something." After he'd said the words, Jin realised every fuck with Mindy had been about this moment with Amy. "I slept with someone."

Amy continued to focus on some distant point, as if the car were driving at an impossible speed and it was taking all her concentration to remain on the road. The silence was excruciating.

"I know," she said.

Jin wondered how he could ever have been unsure of his wife's reaction. She knew. Of course she did. She'd always known. She probably knew before the idea had had a chance to take form inside his head.

"I'm a cliché," he said. He'd had the thought before. And now, as always, he greeted it with a surprised and frustrated disappointment. He was not so different from everyone else.

"You know what's a cliché?" Amy replied. Jin searched for anger in her voice but heard none.

"Cliché is how, after I'd discovered a message on your phone, I found myself folding laundry. Like some kind of unthinking robot." She shook her head, still incredulous. "And not anybody's laundry either. *Your* laundry. Your greying Bonds boxers." She smiled at the memory—one of those smiles that didn't reach the eyes. "I'd just found out you were fucking another woman, and there I was, folding your underwear."

Jin couldn't look at her—couldn't bear to behold the hate, not for him but for herself, in her face.

"That's when I knew I was doomed. Committed for fucking life."

# LUCIE

LUCIE WAS ALONE IN THE HOUSE. HER GRAND-
mother was out back, cleaning up the granny flat, and
her mum was driving to the hospital to pick up her dad,
who was not cold and dead as Lucie had imagined but
very well and COVID-free with the heart of a twenty-
year-old (apparently).

Lucie didn't mind it so much, being alone. In some
ways it was easier, not having to tune in to the mood or
interpret the shifts in the facial expressions of the adults,
who never seemed to say what they meant or mean what
they said. When alone, she found herself gravitating
towards books, and this morning was no different.

She reached across the bed for Pauline's copy of *Watership Down*, which she had rediscovered in the granny flat
and placed on her bedside table. She buried her nose in
the paperback's browned and dusty pages. Her dad had
told her once that dust was actually just human skin, and
so as she inhaled, she imagined some of the cells of her

mother and grandmother floating into her lungs and becoming part of her.

The book was similar to other books Lucie had read. Everybody seemed to be on a journey, traversing dangerous terrain to find treasure—or, in the rabbits' case, safety. Lucie's family, by comparison, seemed stuck. Even before the lockdown, they never really went anywhere. Perhaps they should have been running, Lucie thought. Maybe if they had been running, Ruby wouldn't have died. What had her gran said the other day about a rolling stone gathering no moss? But Lucie also knew that Ruby hadn't been killed by moss. She'd drowned in a bath because her grandmother, who was supervising her, had collapsed. And how would running have helped Pauline escape a stroke, which, from what her dad had told her, was like a little bomb waiting to explode inside her own brain?

Of all of them, her dad travelled the most. Before the pandemic, he would disappear for weeks and come back with new perfumes for her mum and tiny hotel soaps wrapped in waxy paper for Nai Nai and strange toys Lucie didn't really know what to do with, other than put them on the shelf above her bed.

The rabbits in *Watership Down*, by contrast, travelled with purpose, to find a new and suitable home. If Lucie had a choice, she knew which home she would pick. She would pick the house with the letterbox, because it looked finished and tidy and so unlike her own home with its blue tarp and builders' rubble out the front.

Sometimes, when she joined Gran on her evening strolls, Lucie would peer into the house's bright yellow window and see the mother working on her computer and the daughter—whom Lucie recognised from school—sitting on the mother's lap. The mother would be typing with her chin resting on the crown of her daughter's head, and Lucie would feel surprised that the mother didn't look more annoyed.

Lucie read a few pages of the book before replacing the Uno card she was using as a bookmark and slipping on her sandals. Reading about the rabbits always made her want to see Fiver, lie down beside him, run her hands through his fur. But as soon as she opened the back door, as soon as she saw Gran standing beside the hutch with a bent head and fallen shoulders, she knew. Just as she had known when her dad picked her up early from school that awful day, in the middle of PE—when she'd seen him standing, with a pale face and frantic eyes, amidst a flurry of flying balls.

# AMY

AMY DROVE OUT OF THE PARKING LOT AND
headed home. Jin didn't appear well, not at all, but not
because he was gaunt or pale. It was because he looked
small, smaller than she had ever seen him before, as if he
were trying very hard to shrink into himself.

It was this smallness that prevented Amy from feeling angry when he confessed. She had anticipated this
moment, she had fantasised about it, sharpening her words
like blades for maximum damage when it finally came. But
in her imagined confrontations, Jin was defensive, with
cold eyes and a hard mouth, which had made it easy and
even thrilling to wound him. She had never envisaged the
shrinking man who sat beside her, like a gift, in the car.
There was no joy to be had in inflicting pain on *him*.

Instead—and this surprised her—she felt a compulsion to make her own admission. Out of the blue she
remembered a friend from high school who, whenever
Amy asked how she was, would always say "Fine" or

"Great" with a wide (if not convincing) smile, until Amy told her some personal horror story, at which point the high school friend would disclose the awful thing she'd been nursing like a small bird to her breast—a tale far more awful than Amy's own confession.

Amy waited, quiet and patient, giving Jin's secret the space it deserved. And then, once they had pulled into the driveway, she let it go.

"I hate my book."

"The one you're writing?"

"No. The one I published."

She saw shock in Jin's eyes, and this pleased her more than she thought it should.

"Why?"

"Because the entire time I was promoting it, I resented every minute I spent with Ruby. And Lucie. But mostly Ruby. She was so needy. Which sounds ridiculous, of course she was. She was a baby. But I couldn't help how I felt. And I was so happy to fly off to the festival. I kept waiting for the guilt, as I drank coffee watching planes taxi, as I perused the newsagent searching for my book, which wasn't there, and as I waited in line to board, but it never came. Even as I squeezed milk from my breasts into that tiny metallic sink in the restroom on the plane to ease the pain, I felt exhilarated to be away from her. From all of you."

"That's understandable."

"That's what I told myself."

"Totally normal."

"But then the worst possible thing that could have happened, happened. And when I came back, there was no baby to need me and my breasts stopped producing milk and I had all the time in the world, too much time, I was drowning in the minutes and hours and days, and I felt like I had made a deal with the devil, as if he had mistaken one of those thoughts I had sometimes—maybe everybody has them before their conscience kicks in—for a wish. A book for a baby."

She didn't know what she'd expected. Perhaps a sense of release and relief. Perhaps something like her experience of giving birth—an immediate fading of the pain that made her question whether she'd ever experienced the pain at all. And yet she felt nothing.

But then Jin kissed her so hard that her head hit the headrest with a soft thud, and she felt that. And then he put his hands on her cheeks, her neck, her breasts, her belly, her thighs, and she felt that. And then he thrust his warm tongue into her mouth, filling it, and she felt that. And, beneath it all, she felt something else too. Something vague and difficult to place, like a memory. A memory of a dream.

It was a quick and clumsy fuck, the way they had used to fuck, a long time ago, before children and stress incontinence and Jin's vasectomy. They were hungry, as if they couldn't be sure they would ever fuck again. The cabin grew hot with their breath and the chassis rocked. They came together, soundlessly, with their damp eyes squeezed shut.

# PAULINE

SHE COULD SEE THE FLUSH OF SEX ON THEM when they shuffled through the door sometime around 6:00 PM. Lucie, weak from crying, had just passed out on the couch, her messy head on Pauline's lap, her slack lips on Pauline's thigh. Pauline watched her daughter and son-in-law navigate their way as if entering the living room for the first time, crab-walking along the wall and colliding with furniture in an absurd attempt to avoid looking at each other, to avoid brushing up against each other. They were a couple of postcoital teenagers, and the spectacle pleased Pauline more than their union had ever pleased her before.

Sensing loss—as people who have experienced great loss are wont to do—Amy and Jin gathered around the sleeping body of Lucie like campers around a fire. Pauline recounted the discovery of Fiver's disappearance in breathy whispers. She noted the shock on Jin's face—a face that didn't look capable of absorbing many more shocks—and Amy's somewhat muted response.

Without signalling anyone, Pauline cradled Lucie's head in the crook of her left arm and slung her plastered arm beneath Lucie's shoulders. Jin crawled across the rug and scooped up Lucie's torso, her bottom falling neatly in the space between his elbows. Amy cupped a socked heel in each of her hands. They didn't speak but moved intuitively as one unit, as if, like the paramedics who had transferred Ruby from the stretcher to the resuscitation bed, they had performed this procedure countless times before.

Spread as she was across the three of them, Lucie, with her birdlike bones, was almost weightless, and Pauline was reminded of levitation games during childhood sleepovers—the delighted and terrified screams as they raised a friend off the floor with their fingers. How gullible they'd been back then, how willing to *believe*.

Their formation moved down the dimly lit corridor towards Lucie's bedroom at the front of the house. Amy held both of Lucie's heels in one hand and threw the covers wide with her other hand. Together, they lowered Lucie's body down like a plank of wood onto the mattress. Pauline and Jin stepped backwards, silent and solemn pallbearers, but Amy remained perched at the foot of Lucie's bed. Pauline and Jin didn't speak as they retreated—Jin to the master bedroom and Pauline to the living room—but Pauline knew her son-in-law felt the same thing she did. A fragility, as if the air were glass and one word from either of them would shatter it.

# LUCIE

SHE WAS NOT ASLEEP. AT SOME POINT, PROBABLY when they had started touching her, cradling her, elevating her, Lucie had woken from her deep slumber. It was a strange way to rouse but she was not frightened—she was still young enough to remember falling asleep in one place and waking up in another.

They didn't talk as they moved her, but Lucie could tell whose hands belonged to whom. She knew her gran was at her head because she could smell her perfume and feel her breath—that faint wheeze when she lifted anything heavier than a loaf of bread—and she knew her dad was cradling her body because his forearms had a bulk to them, and she knew her mother was holding her feet because of the hesitancy in her grip—her dependence on the strength of the others.

It was a surprise when her mother stayed behind after the others had left, and Lucie wondered if perhaps she knew (had known all along!) that she was faking sleep.

But if she did, she didn't say anything. She simply slid off her shoes, using the toe of one to push off the heel of the other, and slipped beneath the covers.

Lucie felt her mother's skin, always a few degrees cooler than her own, against her bare arm, and it was soothing in the way that a damp towel can be soothing against a wound. She couldn't remember the last time her mother had lain with her like this—perhaps it was when Lucie had been unwell, a long time ago, before the lockdown, when she had been smaller and easier to envelop. It was definitely long enough ago for Lucie to have forgotten the comfort of having her mother coiled around her like a cocoon, an extra layer to absorb the shocks and blows that, Lucie was coming to realise, were a part of living.

# AMY

AMY SLEPT MORE SOUNDLY ON THE NARROW
strip of foam mattress than she had in months. She
woke before Lucie and watched the early morning sun
play with the frayed ends of her daughter's hair. It was
impossible to ignore how alike she and Lucie looked,
especially now, while Lucie was asleep and her eyes—
the dark, intelligent eyes of her father—were hidden
behind her lids.

When Amy was pregnant with Lucie, Pauline had said,
repeatedly (which had irked her), that she had *no idea*
what motherhood would be like. This was, of course,
true, but it was said with such happy superiority that
Amy couldn't help but feel annoyed. *Lots of people have
children*, she would think, angrily, in the hours after
such encounters. *Lots of people less smart and less capable than I am.* But it was not a matter of being smart or
capable; Amy saw that now. It was a matter of being torn

into multiple parts and then standing by as those rogue parts walked the earth, unsupervised and unchaperoned, taunting destiny.

# JIN

THE GRANNY FLAT HAD BEEN STRIPPED. THE
mattress was bare. The bedside table was empty. Stray
books and magazines had been returned to their rightful
places in the house. The only colour against the white
walls and white tiles was the bent form of Pauline, wearing a loose yellow dress and searching the crevices of the
room for anything she might have missed—a hair band,
a pen, an earring—the type of things, forgettable things,
people were forever leaving behind.

She was still wearing the cast on her right wrist, which
reminded Jin that she had been with them for less than
three weeks. It felt longer. Not in a bad way. It was just
that so much had happened: Fiver's illness and disappearance, Jin's admission to the hospital, the break-in. Only
that morning, Jin had received a call from the police
informing him that the prowler had been apprehended.
A kid from the local high school—he'd broken into five
houses in one week and hadn't stolen a thing.

It was easy to forget Pauline was injured, the way she cooked and cleaned and fussed about. Right now, she was on her hands and knees, peering beneath the bed. Jin didn't understand this diligence. Pauline was only returning home, to her house in the outer eastern suburbs. They would probably meet up again soon, maybe even as early as next week.

But then the pandemic had made small distances seem long—and long distances all but infinite. That was why Jin had been so adamant about visiting his parents when the restrictions had lifted. It was only once he was banned from seeing them that he realised it was what he wanted. Now, after the chest-pain scare, he yearned for their company even more.

As Jin waited for Pauline to finish packing, he surveyed the backyard. On arriving home from the hospital with a bill of excellent health, Jin had found himself intolerant of clutter. He had immediately requested a quote from Max's building company to finish repairs on the front of the house. Later, he had searched Airtasker for someone to remove all the junk from the backyard. The dusty piles of bricks were no longer imbued with the promise of a crucial home improvement. The rusting tools were no longer a depressing reminder of an abandoned project. They were just bricks and tools. Which made it easier for Jin to give them away to the man with the orange beard—a nice enough fellow who called himself the Brick Man and drove a purple truck with those very words plastered in tangerine letters across its panels.

His eyes settled on the hutch. It had an expectant air about it, sitting there empty, with its door ajar, in the middle of the backyard. But Jin would never dare suggest getting another rabbit, not now. While Fiver was not one to show his love—did he love them? were rabbits even capable of such a thing?—Lucie had grown attached to him. Sometimes Jin wondered if they didn't love him more for the little surge of dopamine they all felt when, after days of being aloof, he lowered his head for a scratch.

Jin remembered the day Amy had come home from school drop-off, a year (or was it two?) after Ruby died, deathly pale. After several hours of weeping, Jin managed to coax it out of her. Another parent had said: "Will you try for another?" As if Ruby were as replaceable as a microwave or a washing machine. As if, at six months, the little girl hadn't already shown herself to be exceptional. As if another random reassortment of DNA would produce that same melodic giggle-chuckle-snort they'd all loved so much. As if the replacement child wouldn't feel it—the pressure of relentless comparison, the devastating heartbreak of always coming up short.

But a pet was not a child. They were not the same. And people replaced pets, even if there might be a pause for mourning, a period of grace—the length of which depended on the family, and the circumstances of the death. And while Fiver was, strictly speaking, disappeared rather than deceased, Jin was in no doubt that the animal was dead. There was no conceivable way that floppy-eared Fiver, raised in captivity and bred to suit the Northern Hemisphere winter, would know how to survive the city heat and feral cats and native birds of prey. Jin could imagine him trying to hide, because he still had basic instincts, but he would be waiting in vain for his human saviour-captor to arrive with a lettuce leaf and a handful of hay.

Pauline was standing at the door of the flat now, watching him stare at the hutch. She didn't speak, but he knew she knew what he was thinking—she often seemed to, lately. She smiled, and as she did, the sun emerged from behind a clump of cloud to bathe her yellow dress in an even yellower light, and Jin caught a glimpse of his mother-in-law's younger self, and a glimpse of her daughter, his wife. He saw them both, and he saw their beauty.

# LUCIE

LUCIE FELT THE VEHICLE SHUDDER AS THEY
loaded Gran's stuff into the back. Pauline would be
sitting on Ruby's side—after all these years, Lucie still
thought of it this way, as if the car had been divided into
four equal parts, one for each of them. Lucie would never
dream of sitting on Ruby's side, but such things didn't
seem to bother her grandmother. She was always sitting
and standing in places she wasn't supposed to. This, more
than anything, was what Lucie was going to miss when
she was gone. The last thing she wanted was to return
to the long afternoons and silent dinners that had been
their life before Pauline and Fiver.

Lately, she had the sense something had shifted—she
saw it in the way her dad put his hand on the small of
her mum's back as he moved past her in the kitchen, and
in the way her mum stayed at the dinner table long after
they'd finished eating. But life had taught Lucie that
happy moments were like early scenes in a movie, when

everything was going well for the main character. They might be walking (or dancing!) down the street with a light step and a stupid grin while everybody, even the least perceptive members of the audience, knew—based on nothing other than the character's cheerfulness—that something catastrophic was about to happen.

But today Lucie found that the dark images, ordinarily so bold and insistent, were less intrusive. She was able to follow the exceedingly polite conversation between her mum and Gran, and she was even able to look out the window of the car and see what they were passing. And so she saw the way the sun, growing more brazen with the arrival of summer, beamed down upon the bright white weatherboards of all the houses, and she saw how the jacaranda tree near her school had become plump with purple flowers, and she saw the new crimson graffiti tag on the wall of the milk bar—so fresh it was still dripping. And when they turned down one of the more unkempt streets of the neighbourhood, she also saw, amidst a cluster of unpruned daisy bushes, a patch of fur the colour of wheat—not so different from the tuft of golden hair, soft as floating thistle seeds, that had once graced her sister's forehead.

# Acknowledgments

There is only one name on the cover of this book, but there should be many. I am indebted to Clare Forster from Curtis Brown Australia and Michael Heyward from Text Publishing for their enduring support. I am also deeply grateful to the team at Text: Anne Beilby, Emily Booth, Maddy Corbel, and W. H. Chong. It has been a delight to join the Tin House family, and thanks must go to David Forrer from InkWell Management as well as Win McCormack, Masie Cochran, Becky Kraemer, Beth Steidle, Nanci McCloskey, Alyssa Ogi, Elizabeth DeMeo, Anne Horowitz, Allison Dubinsky, Jae Nichelle, and Jacqui Reiko Teruya from Tin House. Thanks, too, to the entire team at Norton. This book would not exist without help from the most important people in my life—Rani, Alyssa, Toby, Mum, Dad, Justin, Sonia, Ibbi, Lawrie, and the Chahal family—you keep me going. And it would be remiss of me not to mention our beloved rabbit: Miles, you can't read, but this book is for you.

# Melanie Cheng

is an award-winning author and doctor based
in Melbourne, Australia.